P9-BZG-956

Bullets punched holes in the fender near Bolan's head

He rolled to the passenger side of the pickup just as the sniper rifle's report boomed again and another round tore through the cargo bed on the driver's side. The flames from the engine would soon engulf the entire truck or reach the gas tank. Neither scenario made for a case to stay put.

Sticking his gun up over the edge of the bed, Bolan cranked off several 3-round bursts, then heaved himself over the side. Falling to the ground, he scooted under the truck, hoping to pick off at least one of the shooters before the sniper got lucky.

He scanned the forest, looking for movement, and caught a flash of fire from the tree line about twenty yards behind the truck.

Then a *whoosh* came from behind him and the engine burst with a spray of fluid. The flames dimmed for a moment, then flared up with renewed intensity. Bolan felt his feet and legs growing hotter each second. He shut all that out, and narrowed his world to the dot inside the circle at the end of the gun.

Amid the chaos, the Executioner inhaled through his nose, let the air escape through his mouth and squeezed the trigger.

MACK BOLAN ®

The Executioner

The Executioner®
Don Pendleton's
NUCLEAR STORM

A GOLD EAGLE BOOK FROM
WORLDWIDE®

TORONTO • NEW YORK • LONDON
AMSTERDAM • PARIS • SYDNEY • HAMBURG
STOCKHOLM • ATHENS • TOKYO • MILAN
MADRID • WARSAW • BUDAPEST • AUCKLAND

First edition February 2012

ISBN-13: 978-0-373-64399-8

Special thanks and acknowledgment to
Travis Morgan for his contribution to this work.

NUCLEAR STORM

Every creature is better alive than dead, men and moose and pine trees, and he who understands it aright will rather preserve its life than destroy it.

—Henry David Thoreau
1817–1862

Human beings have certain rights, the greatest being that to live. And when anyone dares steal this right from innocent people, I will step in and take away that person's rights—every last one.

—Mack Bolan

THE
MACK BOLAN
LEGEND

Nothing less than a war could have fashioned the destiny of the man called Mack Bolan. Bolan earned the Executioner title in the jungle hell of Vietnam.

But this soldier also wore another name—Sergeant Mercy. He was so tagged because of the compassion he showed to wounded comrades-in-arms and Vietnamese civilians.

Mack Bolan's second tour of duty ended prematurely when he was given emergency leave to return home and bury his family, victims of the Mob. Then he declared a one-man war against the Mafia.

He confronted the Families head-on from coast to coast, and soon a hope of victory began to appear. But Bolan had broken society's every rule. That same society started gunning for this elusive warrior—to no avail.

So Bolan was offered amnesty to work within the system against terrorism. This time, as an employee of Uncle Sam, Bolan became Colonel John Phoenix. With a command center at Stony Man Farm in Virginia, he and his new allies—Able Team and Phoenix Force—waged relentless war on a new adversary: the KGB.

But when his one true love, April Rose, died at the hands of the Soviet terror machine, Bolan severed all ties with Establishment authority.

Now, after a lengthy lone-wolf struggle and much soul-searching, the Executioner has agreed to enter an "arm's-length" alliance with his government once more, reserving the right to pursue personal missions in his Everlasting War.

Prologue

Sitting under the clear Wyoming night sky, the thousands of stars overhead giving him an amazing view of the heavens, Joseph Sidell felt the stress of his first graduate student semester finally begin to dissipate from his neck and shoulders.

On the other side of the campfire, his roommate, George Turlington, smiled as he tossed another log on the blaze, making a burst of sparks float into the night sky. "Feelin' better, buddy?"

"Yeah, but I'm still worried about the havoc this trip is gonna wreak on my schedule."

"Jeez, will you just relax for the next two days? MIT will still be there when you get back, and your crushing workload will be right there waiting for you, too. Right now, just sit back, ponder the heavenly light show above us, and—" he winked one deep brown eye "—think of other pleasures you could be enjoying."

Joe frowned. "What are you talking about?"

George rolled his eyes. "Dude, you have *got* to stop drawing all those buildings people will be living in in 2050 and take an occasional look at the world around you—and the people in it. Brandy is *way* into you, man!"

Joe's brow furrowed even more. "Shut up! I wouldn't even have a chance with a woman like her."

"Dude, just 'cause she's got the big brain on campus doesn't mean she doesn't appreciate other things in life—" he pointed a finger at Joe "—unlike some other people I could mention. You know she's into all that environmental save-the-planet stuff. Your little modular boxes you wanna plant on the Serengeti are just the opening you need to start a conversation with her that could lead to—other things."

It was Joe's turn to roll his eyes. Even as an accomplished grad student in quantum physics, George's exploits on campus with the opposite sex—students and professors both—were already the stuff of legend. With his Denzel-like looks, athletic ability and stratospheric IQ, he combined looks, body and brains in a completely irresistible package. Joe figured all his buddy would have to do was say the word and Brandy would fall naked at his feet.

By contrast, Joe was a brown-haired, blue-eyed, fair-skinned German, indistinguishable from any of the thousand other grad students on campus. That Brandy would even give him a second glance when Mr. Adonis was right beside him was an idea Joe found ludicrous at best.

George rubbed a hand over his face and sighed. "Look, I'll prove it to you. When the others come back, I'll bet she'll come up with some excuse to go off for something— firewood, perhaps—and will ask for help. There's your chance, stud."

Joe smiled at his friend's pipe dream. "I think you've been smoking too much salvia, buddy. But all right, just to shut you up, let's see what happens when they return." He looked around the neatly set up campsite, with the tents arranged around the campfire, and folding stadium chairs next to fully stocked coolers. Opening the nearest one, he grabbed a beer from it and raised an eyebrow at his roommate. "While we're waiting…"

"Now you're talking." George deftly caught the cold can Joe tossed to him.

Bright headlights illuminated the clearing as an ancient but well cared-for Jeep Cherokee slowly climbed the narrow road—little more than a trail—leading to the campsite. The diesel engine died, and four students spilled out of the four-by-four.

Joe watched the quartet unload the rest of their supplies and haul them closer to the fire. Sanjay Patel was a mechanical engineering student working on the next generation of rechargeable batteries—and engines. Sandra Talbot was the archetypical mousy, brown-haired, glasses-wearing, library-haunting geek—who also happened to be studying the cutting edge of particle physics and had a 193 IQ. She was also George's current girlfriend, which Joe was still trying to figure out. When he'd asked his roomie about her, all the other guy had said was, "What can I say? I likes 'em with big brains."

Samuel Moskowitz, a finance grad taking a double major in forensic accounting and computer science, was planning to fight Wall Street crime after graduation. Rounding out the sextet was the improbably named Brandy Bodeen.

Even as buried as he was in worrying about the crushing workload awaiting him back at campus, Joe's heart skipped a beat and his jeans tightened when he saw the lithe blonde tote another cooler to the site. Curved in all the right places, and slender everywhere else, she even made her shapeless hoodie and blue jeans look like a model was wearing them.

There were loud greetings, backslaps, and several beer cans cracked open as everyone got down to the serious business of relaxing—namely, drinking until they could barely see. Joe had rejoined the group near the fire and caught George's steady gaze. He shook his head and shrugged, and that was when he heard the words.

"Fire's getting low." Brandy rose gracefully from her cross-legged position on a blanket. "I'm gonna get more wood. Who wants to come with me?"

The others muttered excuses, and with a start Joe realized he was the only one who hadn't spoken yet. "I—I'll go." He scrambled to his feet, trying to avoid tripping or stumbling. As he rose, he saw George wipe a smile off his face and realized what was going on.

Son of a bitch—he set the whole thing up, Joe thought. He tore his gaze away from his roommate only to find himself staring at Brandy, who was looking at him with her round, blue eyes, a faint crease between her eyebrows indicating her puzzlement.

"You ready?" Her lush, full-lipped grin was impish, and at that moment Joe couldn't have cared less if this whole thing had been set up, or it she had been a prostitute instead of one of the smartest minds at MIT. If she wanted to get with him, who was he to refuse?

He smiled back. "Absolutely."

"Hey sport, catch." Joe turned just in time to put his hands up and grab the flashlight Sanjay had tossed to him.

"Don't get lost out there. Stay within sight of the fire," Sam said as he stirred the blaze with a stick.

"Yes, Mom," Brandy replied, cracking up the rest of the group. "Come on, Joe."

Walking beside her, Joe and Brandy left the warm circle of light and entered the forest proper. Joe felt the four pairs of eyes on his back as they left. Moving his finger back behind him, he flipped them all off, making the four howl with laughter again.

Brandy glanced behind them, and Joe quickly turned his bird into scratching an itch. "What was that about?"

"I'm sure George told a joke or something." Joe looked

around as they proceeded deeper into the woods. Birch, ash and oak trees towered over them, mixed with pine and fir, which lent the night a clean, woodsy scent. He was a city boy through and through, but tried not to show his nervousness about being here. His only other experiences with nature had been the science camps his parents had packed him off to every summer. Even then, he'd spent more time indoors doing experiments than the normal things like swimming and fishing that boys did at that age.

Alone with Brandy, Joe was even more tongue-tied than at the campsite. She didn't seem to mind, strolling along like she didn't have a care in the world. Finally, he came up with, "So, how's your research coming?"

She turned to him and smiled, her teeth gleaming in the moonlight. "I could bore you to tears with a ten-minute dissertation on the movement of wave particles in the sixth dimension, but I don't think that's why we're here."

She kept staring at him, making Joe's earlier bravado slip away. "Look, I know George arranged this, but I'll understand if you just want to get the firewood and head back—"

Brandy turned to him, and Joe suddenly felt pressure on the back of his head, and before he could wonder why he was leaning forward, she brought his mouth to hers and kissed him hungrily. Joe put his arms around her slim waist and held her, partly to keep from falling over with surprise, and partly just to get his hands on her. The kiss itself was everything he'd ever fantasized about, and then some. When they parted, he sucked in a breath and just stared at her.

"Joe, who do you think gave him the idea?" She smiled again and pulled away from him. "Come on."

They ran deeper into the woods, finding a narrow path that twisted and turned in the moonlight. When they were both sure they'd be safe from any curious eyes, Brandy stopped and turned to him. "You're the reason I came on this trip, you know."

"Me? Why?"

She smiled that dazzling smile again. "I wanted to get to know you better."

Between the beer—Joe was a relative lightweight in the drinking category—his hormones and the light-headedness from her kiss, he could barely keep up. "Uh, yeah, you hardly know me now."

"Well, what better place to change that?" She walked toward him, and Joe raised his hand as he was about to answer her—or say something—but his mouth stopped working as his fingers encountered her firm breast first. Joe froze, mortified, but Brandy unzipped her hoodie and moved his hand inside to cup her warm flesh through her T-shirt.

"That's a good start. Here…" She turned off the flashlight and stuck it in his back pocket. "It's always more fun in the dark."

Joe could scarcely believe this was happening. His other arm curled around her, and he brought her close for a longer kiss. She was warm and willing, molding herself to him, her sweet-tasting mouth open and tongue and exploring. Her hand stole down to the front of his jeans, which were unmistakably bulging.

Even if George did set this up, it would still be worth it, Joe pondered, all other coherent thoughts fleeing as he lost himself in her touch and taste. He also lost track of time. It could have been minutes or hours, but the next thing he was aware of was being jerked back and squinting as an intense light was shone in his face. Joe tried to put an arm up to shield his vision, but it was grabbed and twisted behind his back and up between his shoulder blades.

"What the—ow! Hey, what's going on?" he asked, blinking fast to try to adjust his vision.

Brandy was also protesting what was going on, and Joe heard, "Get your hands off me, fuckwad—" followed by what sounded like a slap, and her voice fell silent.

"Hey, look, just tell us what the problem is here." Joe's tearing eyes were finally adjusting to the glare, and he could see five figures beyond the spotlight. Next to him, Brandy had a hand to her bruised and cut lip. He bent over to look at her, but her answering glance wasn't scared or surprised—she looked furious.

"The only problem is that you two are in the wrong place at the wrong time." The light was suddenly taken away, and Joe got his first look at the intruders.

The group was unlike anyone he had ever seen. Four men and one woman were all dressed in green, brown and black camouflage fatigues, complete with nylon straps and harnesses crisscrossing their chests and around their waists. Camo face paint covered their cheeks and forehead, giving them an unnerving appearance with their white eyes staring out of a swath of black or green. Each had what looked like night vision goggles pushed up on their heads. They were all armed, too, with the biggest guns Joe had ever seen. With a start, he realized they were Heckler & Koch submachine guns like counterterrorist teams used. Before a few seconds ago, he'd only seen them in the movies.

"Uh, okay, guys, what is this—did we stumble on some kind of Army training exercise or something?"

His question didn't bring the desired response. Instead of an answer, the men and woman all looked around and laughed quietly. One of them turned his head and spit on the ground.

"We're about the farthest thing from Army pigs you'll ever see."

Brandy moved closer to Joe, her hand stealing into his. He felt it tremble, and he gave what he hoped was a reassuring squeeze. "Okay, look, obviously we went a little too far down the path, so we'll just head back to our campsite and let you go on your way—"

"Campsite? What campsite? Where?" one of them asked.

"That's not important—look, we should just be going—" Joe pulled Brandy with him as he tried to turn and go back the way they had come.

The group reacted instantly. Two of them moved to cut the pair off from the path, while the woman grabbed Brandy's hand and twisted it free of Joe's.

"Ow—let go, bitch!" Brandy's arm came up in a roundhouse swing that cuffed her attacker on the side of the head. The blow didn't even stagger her, and the woman glared at Brandy with venom in her eyes.

"That's it." In one fluid movement, she drew the pistol on her hip and aimed it at Brandy's head. "This whore dies now—"

"Stand down, Zeta!" the group leader ordered. "No unsilenced shots, remember?"

The woman's lip curled in a snarl, then she raised the pistol and brought it down in a savage blow to Brandy's cheek. The butt of the gun split her skin, making the young woman fall with a scream.

"Hey, what the fuck!" Joe crouched next to Brandy and put his arm around her. He felt the flashlight in his back pocket press into his butt, and thought about using it as a weapon, but dismissed the idea—they'd cut him down before he even got close. "Hey, you all right?"

She looked up at him with unfocused eyes filled with fear. Her once-high, proud cheekbone was gashed to what looked like the bone, bleeding profusely as it started to swell. "Joe," she whispered, "they—they're gonna kill us!"

"You may be right," he whispered. "Just follow my lead, and be ready to run." Joe brought her up with him as he stood again. "Look, we don't know who you are or why you're here, and we don't care. Just—just let us go, and we won't say a word to anyone, I swear. Hell, we'll pack up right now and head home. You'll never see us again."

The group leader grinned without a hint of mirth, making Joe's heart sink. "I wish I could believe that. Hell, if it were up to me, I'd probably let you skedaddle, since it isn't gonna matter one way or the other in a few days anyway." Again, Joe was surrounded by those quiet, ominous chuckles as the man slowly shook his head. "But it isn't up to me. We have our orders, and we're gonna carry them out."

"No!" Brandy broke from Joe's side and launched herself at the woman, hands outstretched to claw at her face.

"Brandy!" Joe could only watch helplessly as the woman intercepted her with a feral smile. She raised her left hand to sweep Brandy's arms away from her face and brought her right hand around from behind her back, shoving it out at the other woman's abdomen.

Brandy stopped as though she had run into a wall. Her mouth fell open, but no sound came out as she slowly looked down at herself.

"I hope that felt as good to you as it did to me." The woman called Zeta did something Joe couldn't see, but it made Brandy's entire body convulse. She then lifted the frozen girl's face up and kissed her open mouth. "Mmm—I never tasted the last breath of anyone before. Kinda sweet."

"Damn, Zeta, that's cold," a tall, skinny man muttered.

"What. Delta said no shots fired. I'm just following orders." The woman took her hand away and stepped back. Brandy turned to Joe, hands clutching her middle, and he saw her waist and legs were dark and wet.

"Oh my God—Brandy! Brandy! What the fuck—" Joe grabbed her as she staggered and fell, easing her to the ground and placing her on her back. As he did, he moved her hands aside and saw a gush of blood well from the wound in her stomach. "What the fuck did you do to her?"

"I stabbed an uppity bitch, that's what I did." Zeta knelt next to him and wiped her bloody blade on Brandy's jeans. "She'll bleed out in a day or two, and be in the most unimaginable agony the whole time. It'd be better if you let one of them put a bullet in her brain."

"Joe…please don't…please don't leave me." Brandy's eyes were huge white pools of terror. She shook again, grabbing his jacket with bloody hands. "I'm cold—so cold."

"Oh, fuck this." Before Joe could do anything, Zeta reached out and drew her blade across the wounded girl's throat. More blood gushed out, and she made horrible choking noises as she died in Joe's arms.

The woman cleaned her blade off again and stood. "Trust me, you should really be thanking me—"

Joe saw red. A howl of fury burst from his throat, and he lunged into the woman, knocking her off balance and sending her tumbling into the men behind her. Whirling, he rushed at the two blocking the path, catching them both by surprise. As they scrambled to bring up their weapons, Joe drew the flashlight from his back pocket and swung it at the nearest man's head, the plastic housing making a satisfying *thunk* as it connected with his skull. The man staggered under the blow, and Joe shoved him into his partner as he took off into the woods, hearing urgent orders behind him.

"No open shooting!"

"Stop him!"

"Sigma, Theta, go! Execute scorched earth!"

Joe ran like the Devil himself was behind him, stumbling along the path leading through the dark forest. The trail, which had seemed wide and clear earlier, was now a twisting, narrow ribbon of dirt under his feet. Branches clutched at his arms and clothing, and an exposed root caught his foot and made him hit the ground and bite his tongue. Tasting blood, he spit it out as he leaped to his feet and kept going, limping now on a twisted ankle. He tried to look around to see if the camouflaged crazies were chasing him or what, but all he saw was black forest, trees trunks rising everywhere like a huge fence, their branches looking like skeletal fingers reaching for him.

Joe knew they couldn't have gone more than a half mile at the most, but his journey back seemed to be a marathon. Every time he thought he'd round one more turn and find the clearing and campsite, he only saw more dark trail. At last, however, he saw the welcoming glow of the fire. Trying to shout, but too winded to do anything more than wheeze, Joe staggered out of the woods toward the laughing and drinking group, which hadn't noticed him yet.

George was the first to spot him lurching from the darkness. "Hey, the prodigal architect returns! Hey, buddy, you all right?"

Joe nearly fell as he tried to reach his roommate, going down to one knee as he fought for breath. He held out his hands, still sticky with Brandy's blood. "Help—please—"

"What the fuck happened, Joe?" George held him up as the rest of the group clustered around, their questions flying.

"Did you guys have an accident?"

"Is Brandy injured?"

"Where is she?"

Joe labored to talk in between breaths. "She's…she's dead, and we're next…killers…in the forest…coming after me—"

"What the hell are you talking about, Joe? And where the hell's Brandy?"

Joe grabbed George's down vest and pulled him close.

"She's dead, goddamnit! And we're next if we don't get outta here right fucking now!"

"Holy shit, you're serious, aren't you—" George had straightened and was looking around when Joe heard a strange noise, like cloth tearing. He looked up to see George staring at him with unfocused eyes, a small hole in his forehead leaking a trickle of red down his face. His roommate fell backward onto the fire, making Sandra scream as his body started burning.

"Oh shit—they're here!" Joe sank to his knees as he realized what he'd done. "I led them right to you."

Sanjay and Sam ran for the Jeep, while Sandra tried to pull George's body from the fire. Joe looked back to see two camouflaged men appear from the woods and track the two running students. He heard that strange ripping cloth noise again, and both Sanjay and Sam fell to the ground near the Jeep, motionless. One of the men peeled off toward the two fallen students, while the other headed toward the fire.

Falling into shock, Joe could only watch as the man approached the fire and put a quick burst of bullets into Sandra's chest. She flung up her arms and fell across George's burning body in the fire, which was popping and crackling in the flames, the stench of burning flesh making his stomach clench. Through his numbness, Joe heard the tearing cloth sound again, and slowly looked over to see the far man putting bullets into the heads of his friends.

"Sorry, man." Joe looked up into the muzzle of the automatic weapon pointed at him, the masked man holding it shaking his head. "Just in the wrong place at the wrong time."

The end of the submachine gun spit fire at his face, and Joe knew nothing more.

1

Four days earlier

Mack Bolan strode through the luxurious casino floor of
the Marina Bay Sands Singapore, oblivious to the bells
and clatter of sophisticated slot machines and the chatter
and exclamations of well-dressed men and women trying
their luck at dozens of gaming tables. His feet sank into
soft, plush carpet, while attractive staff served drinks to
the high rollers, but he ignored all of the activity, his eyes
alert for just one man.

Dressed in a tan sport coat, black short-sleeved shirt and
navy slacks, Bolan blended easily into the crowd of na-
tives and foreign tourists, despite his height and imposing
presence. The clothes were brand-new—mainly because
his luggage had been lost by one of the six airlines he had
been on in the past four days, and was presently at least
twenty-four hours and several thousand miles behind him.
Bolan himself felt edgy from two weeks of nearly constant
travel, all in pursuit of one man.

Kim Dae-jung was a renegade nuclear scientist who'd
defected from North Korea after working ten years at the
highest levels of that country's nuclear program. The U.S.
had mounted an audacious, top-secret mission to free him,

only to suffer the embarrassment of having him give the slip to his handlers and walk out of his hotel in Sydney, Australia. Since then, he'd been traveling around the world, freely spending the ten million he'd stolen from the North Korean government, rarely staying more than one night in the same place, and being chased by an assortment of agents and operatives from several nations, including assassins from his homeland who were tasked with assuring Dae-jung took any military and national secrets to his grave.

Despite his flamboyant style—he favored Dom Perignon champagne and the most expensive luxury suites in every hotel he'd been at—the diminutive Korean had the devil's own luck, escaping government dragnets in several countries. The President had contacted Stony Man Farm and requested that Hal Brognola see if Bolan was available to perform an extraction on short notice.

Along with much of the American intelligence community, Bolan considered North Korea to be one of the largest threats to U.S. security, second only to China. The knowledge inside Dae-jung's head could give analysts invaluable insight into that country's nuclear program. After hearing from the big Fed, Bolan had been on a flight to Australia in three hours.

From there it had a bewildering tour of cities around Southeast Asia. He'd picked up the high-rolling scientist's trail in Port Moresby and had missed him by three hours in Manila. From there, Bolan had passed through the glitter of Hong Kong, Tokyo and Bangkok, until they all blurred together in swaths of neon and steel, mirrored skyscrapers and plush hotels. Every time he landed, he was just one step behind the man. Along the way, he'd crossed paths and swords with men and women from British and Russian intelligence, as well as at least two hit teams, one from North Korea and a Chinese group. Brognola and Bolan figured they wanted the scientist dead before he could reveal China's sales of enriched plutonium and other nuclear material to the regime.

This luxury hotel was the best lead and the closest he'd been to Dae-jung so far.

The soldier finished his sweep and found an unoccupied table at the bar, ordering a ginger ale from the server who magically appeared at his elbow. "I've canvassed the entire casino floor. Plenty of whales swimming in this ocean, but Dae-jung isn't one of them."

His words were transmitted through a tiny, flesh-colored microphone glued to the base of his jaw. They were then sent through a relay of satellites back to Stony Man Farm in Virginia, and the gruff answering voice of Hal Brognola came back to him through an equally tiny earpiece in his right ear. Both communication devices were slaved to the smartphone holstered at his belt, which provided power and a signal boost as well as high-level encryption for both sides of the conversation, ensuring no eavesdroppers.

"If he's not there, he's probably in his room. Have you identified any hostiles on-site yet?"

"None I can see—if they are around, they're staying out of view."

Brognola chuckled. "Easier for them than you, eh, Striker?"

Even through his fatigue, Bolan smiled. "Yeah—unless I'm crouching, it's hard for me to blend in. Do we know which room he's in? There are a lot of suites in the hotel, and I'd rather not kick in the wrong door if I can help it."

"Akira says a man matching Dae-jung's description is staying in the Chairman Suite on the fifty-fourth floor. He's working on getting you access to the secure elevators as we speak."

Bolan drained his ginger ale in one long drink and set the empty glass on the table. "Tell Akira he's got about three minutes to open those doors." Rising, he walked toward the casino's main doors, which slid open at his approach, the air-conditioned comfort giving way to the oppressive mugginess of Singapore at the beginning of monsoon season. The air was thick and humid, and Bolan quickened his pace across the pedestrian bridge. "The vehicle I requested is in place?"

"In the parking ramp, ground floor, space A3."

"So all I have to do is head up there, drag Dae-jung out of his hidey-hole, bring him down with me, get to our vehicle and drive to the airport."

"When you say it, Striker, it sounds almost reasonable. Sorry we couldn't do anything about getting you a sidearm before you went over."

Bolan shrugged, missing the familiar weight of his Desert Eagle under his arm. "If this guy's traveling with the entourage you say he is, I doubt it would get past his bodyguards, and since I'm supposed to be doing this on the down low, well, the .44 is a bit conspicuous. Don't worry— I'm sure I'll think of something."

"Whenever you say that, that's exactly when I start worrying." Bolan heard crunching in his ear and grinned, knowing Brognola had just popped one of his ever-present antacid tablets into his mouth. "However you manage to get him out, just don't create an incident with the Singaporean government. It's bad enough we snuck you in. I'd hate to see us trying to extradite you from one of their prisons."

"Thanks for the pep talk." Bolan entered the main lobby of the Marina Bay, which was decorated to look like a jungle oasis had sprung up in the middle of the huge room, with palm trees and bright orchids and ferns growing inside a walled garden, complete with a twenty-foot waterfall. The rest of the room was modern, covered in exotic hardwoods and marble.

"Okay, walk straight through the lobby and take a right on the far side. The private elevators to the towers will be straight ahead." The voice in his ear was younger and quicker, and Bolan could hear the tinny beat of the constant rock music Stony Man Farm's computer hacker, Akira Tokaido, always listened to when on the job.

"You get that pass worked out yet?" he asked.

"I've almost got it. The security suite in this place is impressive, and coming from me, that's saying something," Tokaido said.

Bolan reached the far end of the room and turned right as instructed. Two sets of gleaming, stainless-steel elevator doors faced him several yards away. Not breaking stride, he headed for them. "Five yards away, Akira. You better type faster."

"Don't you worry, I'm on it." When Bolan was a step away from the nearest set of doors, they slid soundlessly open.

He stepped into a cylinder large enough to hold a dozen people. The doors closed behind him, and the button for floor 57 lit up. The elevator began ascending so smoothly Bolan could hardly tell it was moving. "They spared no expense for this place."

"Yeah. Too bad you won't have a chance to catch a meal there. The restaurants are supposed to be terrific."

Bolan watched the floor numbers tick off. "You'll have to tell me all about it when you're here."

"On my salary? Hardly. Okay, you're coming up to it. The suite will be to the right, the second door on your left. It'll be easy to spot—it's the one with the two bodyguards out front."

"He couldn't have taken a suite near the elevator, could he?"

"Come on. You wouldn't want this to be too easy, would you? I'm cutting in an empty loop of the security camera on that floor. You know how you're gonna get inside?"

"I'll figure something out." The elevator chimed softly,

announcing he'd reached his destination. Bolan stepped out and looked both ways down the hall. Sure enough, two massive men wearing tuxedoes stood at ease in front of the second door on the left. Bolan headed straight for them.

The pair eyed him as he approached, their postures turning from relaxed to alert the closer he got. Bolan stopped in front of the nearer one, a Samoan man built like a mountain, with dark skin and black hair falling in ringlets to his shoulders. Despite his head-crushing demeanor, his voice was smooth and polite, with a hint of British prep school in it. "May I help you?"

Bolan decided to return the politeness. "I'm here to see Dr. Kim Dae-jung."

The bodyguards exchanged glances, and the far one turned to face Bolan, stepping in front of the door. "I'm afraid there is no one inside by that name. Perhaps you have the wrong room."

Bolan held his arms out enough so the hired muscle could see he wasn't packing. "Relax, guys, I'm not carrying. If you'll allow me…" He took out a slim leather billfold and flipped it open. "Matt Cooper, U.S. State Department. Now I know Dr. Dae-jung is inside, and all I'll need is a few minutes of his time." Bolan and Brognola had come up with the State Department cover together, figuring a bureaucrat would be less fearsome than a CIA officer or even the lesser-known U.S. Diplomatic Security Service.

The Samoan examined the credentials for more than thirty seconds. Bolan wasn't concerned—they were real as far as anyone outside the State Department was concerned. "One moment, sir." The bodyguard touched his earpiece and muttered something in what sounded like Korean.

Moments later, the bodyguard returned his attention to Bolan. "Please stand with your legs shoulder-width apart and spread your arms." Bolan complied, and the second man ran a handheld metal detector over his body. When he was finished, the Samoan patted him down thoroughly. Satisfied that Bolan was unarmed, the second bodyguard produced a key card and swiped it through the lock on the double mahogany door, which opened to a burst of music, loud conversation in several languages, the laughter of men and women, and a swirl of smoke.

The Samoan opened the door farther for Bolan. "The doctor will be with his guests in the main room. You will be escorted at all times while inside. Do you have any questions?"

Bolan shook his head and stepped into a small foyer. He was met by a smaller Asian man, also dressed in a tuxedo, with alert eyes, a buzz cut and an unmistakable bulge under his right arm. "If you'll follow me, sir." He turned and escorted Bolan into the large main room.

The huge Chairman Suite more than lived up to its name. It was decorated in black wood and granite, with dark hardwood floors covered with large patterned rugs. A long black-and-silver screen depicting a flock of cranes taking off from a pond took up the far wall of the room. The furniture was modern and sleek, from the leather wingback chairs and plush couches scattered around the room to the ebony baby grand piano surrounded by several women as someone played what sounded to Bolan like some kind of show tune. The women were all singing in more than one language.

From the looks of it, the party had been going on for some time. A long, granite-topped table along one wall contained the remains of a demolished buffet, and suit jackets, evening wraps and shoes were scattered around the room. Bolan guessed the women in attendance were professionals, and as he was led deeper inside, he saw one of them lead a balding, potbellied man dressed only in an undershirt, socks and garters into another room and close the door.

Cigarette and marijuana smoke mingled, the thick, stale cloud obscuring what would probably have been a magnificent view of the city's skyline.

The third bodyguard led Bolan to a corner of the main room, where a large, U-shaped black leather couch was currently hosting several men and women, all in various states of undress. And in the middle of it all, leading his inebriated guests in an off-key chorus of "I Did it My Way" was the man himself, Dr. Kim Dae-jung.

The man known as the driving force behind North Korea's nuclear weapons program wasn't much to look at. Barely clearing five feet, he was pudgy, with a bulging belly that attested to a life spent at a lab table. He wore rimless glasses and his receding black hair, normally swept back from his forehead, stuck out in all directions, as if he had just been mildly electrocuted.

Bolan stood patiently next to the bodyguard while Dae-jung and his group finished their song. His eyes and ears, however, were cataloging every person, where they were, and what they were holding or doing. He spotted two more obvious bodyguards in the room, and one of the prostitutes who he thought might be disguised to blend in with the guests.

The song finished to cheers, applause and everybody drinking a round of what smelled like sake. The bodyguard slipped over to Dae-jung's shoulder and whispered in his ear.

"What? Here? Now? What does he want?" the drunken doctor bellowed. The bodyguard pointed to Bolan, and Dae-jung adjusted his glasses as he looked the soldier up and down. "Well, you State bastards finally caught up with me, didn't you. Took you long enough."

"I'm afraid so, Doctor, although following your trail was

very…interesting. I'd like to talk to you about your accompanying me to the United States, where there are several people who are waiting to talk to you."

Dae-jung peered at him blearily through the smudged lenses of his askew glasses. "I could have you killed, you know. It would be a great mystery. You walk into this room, but you never walk out."

Although he was sure he could take out both of obvious and covert bodyguards without receiving a scratch, Bolan nodded. "You could, but the State Department would just send someone else to find you. Why not save both your bodyguards the trouble of disposing of me, and the U.S. government the trouble of flying someone else halfway around the world, and just come with me now?"

The diminutive scientist stared at Bolan for a few seconds, then roared with laughter. "I've never met a suit with a sense of humor before. Sit, sit, have a drink. You want anything else—a woman, a man, a boy, coke, hash, dust?"

Bolan slid in between Dae-Jung and the beautiful, almost-passed-out Filipino woman next to him. "I've only come for one person. Now that I've found him, it's time to go."

Dae-Jung poured sake into two cups, his hand trembling slightly. He looked several years older than the CIA's most recent picture of him. Bolan wasn't sure if that was due to the stress of being on the run, or due to living a 24/7 party lifestyle for the past few weeks.

Dae-jung picked up one of the glasses and stared into the liquor as if he might be able to see the answer to his problems in it. "I worked for those bastards and our glorious leader for twenty-four years, always maintaining the party line. I did all right, too—cars, summer homes, even vacations. But when my daughter and her entire family starved to death in 2008, well, there's only so much a man can turn a blind eye to, right?"

Bolan nodded. "I would agree with that."

Dae-jung suddenly held out the sake cup to him. "Before I agree to anything, you must drink with me. Otherwise, I will order my bodyguards to have you killed." His smile said he was joking, while his eyes, suddenly clear and piercing, said he wasn't.

Bolan accepted the glass and held it up. "To your daughter and her family—may they rest in peace."

The drunk scientist clinked his glass against Bolan's, spilling a rivulet of liquid down the side, then downed the shot in one gulp. Bolan followed suit, feeling the smooth rice wine heat his palate as it slid down his throat. He placed the empty glass back on the table and watched Dae-jung.

"Can I stay in Las Vegas? I've always wanted to see Las Vegas!" the doctor proclaimed loudly as he grabbed a magnum bottle of champagne and refilled his glass.

"I'm sure that can be arranged." Always aware of the bodyguard, Bolan leaned closer to the small Korean. "However, it would be in your best interest if we were to leave now. Doubtless there are others who are looking for you as well who don't have your well-being in mind, and if I was able to find you, they will soon, too."

Dae-jung swigged his champagne, a drop trickling down his chin. "I'll party tonight, then go with you tomorrow morning, sleep on the flight over."

"With all due respect. Doctor—" Bolan was interrupted by Tokaido's voice in his ear.

"Striker, you've got armed men coming down the hall—shit, they just took out both guards outside the door! They're gonna be inside any second!"

2

Bolan was already standing, trying to lift the drunken scientist to his feet as the bodyguard pushed through the crowd of women to intercept him.

"Hostiles are outside. You'd better check the door!" The bodyguard frowned at Bolan's orders, but the big man wasn't deterred. "Get over there now!"

The guard's indecision cost him dearly. As his gaze flicked to the door, the woman Bolan had pegged as an undercover bodyguard drew a dagger—apparently ceramic, to bypass the metal detector—from a secret compartment in the bottom of her small purse, stepped behind the bodyguard and slit his throat. The man clasped both hands to his spurting neck as he sank to the floor, already dying. The woman bent over him, her hand darting inside his tux jacket for his pistol.

As men and women reacted to the cold-blooded murder, some screaming, others trying to get out of the way, Bolan stepped toward the Asian assassin and snapped a kick into her face like he was punting a football. The woman arched backward as she flew through the air, blood flying from her crushed nose. She landed on an ottoman and slid off, out cold.

Bolan moved to the dead bodyguard, scooped up the

dagger from the carpet and drew the man's pistol, a compact HK P-2000. He drew the slide back just as there was a commotion at the door—a sound like tearing cloth, followed by the crunch of splintering wood. The Executioner walked to the doctor, who was looking around befuddled as his party disintegrated into chaos. "What's happening?"

Bolan didn't reply. He grabbed him by his silk shirt and hauled him over the back of the couch, climbing over it and crouching as the sound of silenced gunfire could be heard on the other side of the room. More screams and shouts followed, along with angry commands yelled in Mandarin, then Korean, then English.

"Nobody move! Stand up! Everyone keep your hands where I can see them!"

Hearing the shouted orders, the confused doctor raised his hands and tried to stand, but was pulled back down by Bolan. "Doctor, I'm going to need you to stay here for the moment, all right?"

"Sure, Mister...whatever you say."

Bolan kept one ear on what was going on in the rest of the room while he contacted Tokaido. "They're inside, multiple gunmen. Can you give me a sitrep on where they are in the room?"

"Negative, Striker. I counted four gunmen in the hallway, but there are no cameras inside the suite. No one's outside but the dead guards, so they must all be in there. I'm afraid that's all the data I have right now."

Crawling to the edge of the long couch, Bolan peeked out just enough to see two pairs of combat boots walking up and down a line of dress shoes, high heels and lots of bare feet. He couldn't see the second pair of shooters, but muffled screams and shouts gave him a pretty good idea of where they were. More threats and the smack of a fist or gun butt on flesh were followed by crying and the addition of more feet on the floor, leaving Bolan with an even bigger problem—if he tried to take out the gunmen, there was a good chance he might hit one of the partygoers. While the chances were excellent that none of the attendees were completely innocent, as far as he knew none had done anything to warrant getting killed on this night either. But without being able to see where the gunmen were standing, it was too risky to engage them. The last thing Bolan wanted was a bloodbath in the opulent suite.

"Where's the doctor? You have one minute to produce him, or we will shoot one of you each minute he's not brought out."

Hearing this, the doctor started to stand again, but Bolan pulled him back down. "Let me go—" he said before Bolan clamped a hand over his mouth.

"You have to stay down and keep quiet!" Dae-jung tried to move his head, fumbling at Bolan's fingers. "Are you going to stay here and be quiet?" The doctor nodded, so Bolan took his hand away.

"I'm not going to let innocent people die because of me!" he whispered.

"I'm not either, Doctor, but you have to trust me." Spotting the edge of the floor screen next to the couch, Bolan got an idea. "Please, just stay here for another minute. If I get killed, you can do whatever you want, okay?"

"Okay."

Bolan began edging behind the screen, which was only a few inches from the hotel room wall. He couldn't move very fast without risking bumping into his cover, which would most likely get the screen and him both stitched with bullets.

"Fifteen seconds! Where is he?" the threat and demand was repeated in Korean and Chinese.

Bolan shimmied behind the screen as fast as he dared. When he reached the second one from the end, he stopped and pressed the tip of the ceramic blade to the cloth in front of him.

"Time's up! You, come here! Get over here!" Bolan heard the smack of a fist or hand striking flesh, and gritted his teeth as he slowly drew the knife down to make a slit big enough to see through. When he put his eye to it, however, all he saw was a herringbone pattern.

One of them was standing right in front of him! However, Bolan immediately realized that wasn't a problem, but a stroke of good fortune. Quickly he enlarged the slit until he could see the back of the man's head.

"All right, last chance! Where is Dae-jung? Fine—she dies now!"

Bolan slipped the barrel of his pistol through the slit, the muzzle only an inch from the man's skin. Placing the ceramic blade between his teeth and his free hand on the screen, he squeezed the trigger.

As soon as the shot went off, Bolan shoved the screen over, the ruined artwork falling on the dead gunman. Instantly he took in the scene. A group of about thirty partygoers huddled against the wall, with three gunmen in the room, two standing a few feet behind the leader, who had an Asian woman in a crimson slit sheath dress next to him, a pistol at her temple. As Bolan had expected, the three shooters stared at him with wide eyes, having been taken by surprise at their partner's head suddenly exploding and spraying blood and brains all over them.

Also, as Bolan had hoped, except for man with the hostage, he had a perfect line of sight on the other two killers.

He lined up his pistol on the farthest one and shot him in the head, then tracked the second one and put two into his chest as he was bringing around his submachine gun. Both bodies dropped to the floor before the sound of Bolan's shots died away.

That left him and the lead hit man, who was using the woman as a shield. "Don't move or she dies!"

Bolan was pretty sure he could take out the man without getting the woman killed, but movement near the attacker's foot caught his attention. The Samoan, his chest stained red from his wounds, was pulling his bulk along in the hallway. He left a thick red trail behind him, but was almost close enough to grab the man. He just needed a few more seconds.

Bolan kept his pistol trained on the small part of the gunman's face that he could see. "I don't want anyone else to die, but I can't let you take the doctor out of here either."

"He's not going anywhere." The hit man was starting to aim his pistol at Bolan when the Samoan plunged a butterfly knife into his target's foot. The man screamed and his pistol went off target as he shoved the woman away and turned to shoot his attacker. He never got the chance.

Bolan squeezed the trigger of his HK pistol once. The .40 caliber bullet cored the hit man's head, spraying the people nearest to him with more bits of bone and brain matter as the corpse fell to the floor, causing a few screams and cries from several women.

The Executioner was moving before the body landed, walking to one of the men and grabbing his submachine gun, an oversized pistol with a second handle that he recognized as a Brugger & Thomet MP-9. Both of the covering gunmen were armed with the same weapon and carried a spare 30-round magazine. Bolan tucked the HK into the small of his back and grabbed everything, tucking the spares into the pockets of his suit jacket. Then he ran back to the couch and got the scientist on his feet.

"Time to go, sir."

"If you say so." Keeping one of the TMPs ready, Bolan had slung the other one over his shoulder and used his free hand to support Dae-jung as they headed for the door. The doctor pasted a smile on his face and addressed the group. "I thank you all for coming, and suggest that if you don't want to be here when the police show up, you should leave immediately."

"Two minutes after we're gone." Bolan added, seeing several of the guests edging toward the door. One look at him and the lethal-looking submachine gun in his hand, and they all stopped in their tracks.

Bolan kept moving the Korean toward the door, stepping around the motionless Samoan. Dae-jung gasped when he saw the huge body. "Felipo's dead?"

"Afraid so. If it makes you feel any better, he died saving my life." Bolan pushed the double doors open and used the one closest to the elevator as a shield, peeking around it to scout the hallway.

"Akira, what's the security situation?"

"You sure stirred up a hornet's nest, Striker—"

"I didn't bring the guns to this party, but I'm damn sure gonna use them to clear the way out. What's the best route to get to the garage?"

"They're putting men on every elevator. Can you take the stairs?"

Bolan glanced at Dae-jung, whose head lolled on his shoulders as he stared at his rescuer. "Negative. Target is in no condition to run down fifty-four flights."

"Then you'll probably want to ambush the two guards coming out of the first car, and grab that one. They'll be there in about fifteen seconds."

"This job just keeps getting better and better," Bolan gritted, hauling the scientist toward the elevator.

He'd just reached the alcove when he heard the soft chime indicating the car's arrival. Bolan propped the doctor up against the wall. "Stay here." The Korean waved at him weakly as Bolan ran into the alcove, passing the door to stand on the other side. He got there just as the doors opened and two security guards ran out, hands on their holstered pistols. Bolan stepped out and aimed his subgun at them. "Freeze!"

Both men whirled, then raised their hands when they saw Bolan had the drop on them. He pointed at the ground. "Lie on the ground, hands on your heads!"

The two men complied. "Better hurry, Striker—a lot more are coming."

"Going as fast as I can." Bolan ran over to them and removed their pistols, tossing them down the hallway. Grabbing Dae-jung, he hurried the man into the elevator, making sure the guards' eyes were staring at the polished marble floor. Bolan stabbed the button for the garage. "I hope you've overridden all the security on this cage."

"Of course. What did you think I'd been doing while you were rubbing elbows with the high and mighty? You should be reaching the lowest level in approximately twenty seconds."

"Got it. Hey, are you all right?" he asked Dae-jung, who was leaning against the elevator wall, breathing rapidly. His face was pasty, and a sheen of sweat had broken out on his forehead.

"I don't—I don't feel so well."

"Given how much booze you put away, I'm not surprised. We're going to a vehicle in the garage, and from there to the airport, where a plane is waiting to take you back to the United States. Just a half hour or so, and we'll be in the air."

"I'll believe it when I see it."

"You will soon enough." The elevator dinged, and Bolan grabbed Dae-jung's shoulder and supported him as they exited, walking out into a nondescript corridor. "What the hell, Akira? Where's the garage?"

"Those elevators don't go directly to the parking levels. You'll need to turn right and go approximately forty yards.

There will be a door marked like the one on your smartphone that should give you access to the garage level."

Bolan began jogging down the hallway, half-carrying, half-dragging the semiconscious scientist along with him.

"Turn at the next door on your right."

Bolan did so and was rewarded with the bare concrete minimalism of the hotel's garage.

"The vehicle is on this level, Bay C halfway down the aisle, a green Toyota Harrier SUV," Tokaido said.

"Good, I have a feeling I might need the room." Bolan checked for any movement or active vehicles on the level before hauling Dae-jung out with him and crossing to the closest concrete pillar. He had just reached it when the roar of a motorcycle shattered the silence. The driver revved his engine, the echo making it almost impossible to tell where it was coming from.

Bolan looked around for a map, and saw he had reached Bay B. "Doctor, we have to go a little further to reach my car. You still with me?"

"I think so…unless I throw up first…" The Korean scientist's face had taken on a gray pallor, and his eyes had become even more unfocused.

"It's just a few more yards. Hang on a bit longer and then you can rest. Here we go."

Still supporting the semiconscious man with his free hand, Bolan kept the MP-9 ready as they started to cross the next bay. The moment they passed the immaculate black Bentley on the other side, a bright light turned on, illuminating Bolan and his charge in its halogen light. Before he could blink or aim, the light leaped forward as the motorcycle shot straight for them, the helmeted driver extending a pistol to shoot as he zoomed by.

3

If he'd been alone, Bolan would have moved to intercept the motorcyclist and take him out, but his first goal had to be protecting Dae-jung.

He whipped the other man around, shielding him with his body as he drove him to the floor. At the same time, he brought up the MP-9 and fired a burst in the bike's general direction. Bolan wasn't expecting to hit anything, but he figured the surprise of finding out his prey was armed might spoil the rider's aim.

He was right. The gunman's nerve broke as Bolan's weapon spit rounds near him. Swerving, he almost lost control of his blue-and-white street bike, the back wheel fishtailing on the smooth concrete floor, but pulled it out at the last second and zoomed around the ramp. His pistol shots, however, went wild.

As soon as the biker was completely past, Bolan hauled Dae-jung to his feet. "We've got to move!" Even as he said that, however, another single headlight lit them both up, and the garage level reverberated with the roar of the motorcycle coming at them again.

Before Bolan could even think about crossing the few yards of empty space between them and the next lot, the biker was on them, his pistol spitting bullets.

Bolan did the only thing he could do—he heaved Dae-jung over the hood of the Bentley and dived after him, hoping they both would get to cover before any of the bullets found them. He heard the thunks as the lead punched through the fender of the luxury car they hid behind. As he landed on the concrete, Bolan caught a glimpse of a yellow-and-red motorcycle racing by, its rider snapping off a shot that smacked into the low concrete wall at the head of the row, just above Bolan's head, showering him with dusts and rock chips.

"Are we there yet?" Dae-jung asked, looking around.

"Not quite."

Two shooters! Bolan had to admire the relative neatness of the trap they were in. With both ends blocked, no matter how he tried to advance or retreat, Bolan and Dae-jung would always be facing one or both of the bikers. Even with his submachine gun, the bikes were fast and maneuverable in the enclosed space, canceling almost all of the advantage of a fully automatic weapon.

The bikes roared again, preparing to make another run-and-gun pass. Bolan glanced at the vehicle behind them, a Lexus luxury SUV with a relatively high ground clearance. His plan formed instantly.

"Doctor, I need you to hide under here for a bit." Bolan shoved him under the SUV.

With a strained gasp, the Korean disappeared under the SUV. Bolan hit the ground as well, trying to figure out which biker would be coming for them first.

"What the hell's going on?" Tokaido asked.

"I've got two trigger-happy motorcyclists trying to take us both out in the garage!" Bolan snapped. "They've got us pinned down in Bay B."

"Oh, yeah, I see 'em. Looks like the one above you is about to make another pass."

"You can see him? How far away is he?"

"Yeah, I'm hacked into the security cams. He's about twenty yards from you. What does that have to—"

"Perfect! Hold on!" Bolan dropped to his stomach and crawled under the Lexus, bracing his MP-9 with both hands in front of him. The bike's engine reached a high point as the rider gunned his throttle, then took off down the ramp.

Bolan gave him a two-count to get up to speed, then squeezed the trigger of his weapon, emptying the magazine. The biker drove straight into the stream of bullets, which chewed up his leg and punched into the bike's engine. Losing control, he spun out and flipped off the street machine, which fell over and crashed into the far wall, pinning the biker between it and the cinder blocks. Bolan rolled out and took aim in case the shooter was coming up for more, but man's body lay unmoving on the floor.

"One down. Where's the other one?" Bolan asked while ejecting the empty magazine and reloading.

"At the bottom of the ramp on your six. He seems uncertain—he's not moving forward yet."

"Good. Let me know if he starts moving in the next three seconds." Still keeping an eye on the downed rider, Bolan moved around the back of the Bentley, crouched and crept forward until he was next to the concrete barrier. There was a chain link fence on the end.

"He's starting to move—now!"

Bolan took a deep breath, centered himself and steadied his hands on the MP-9. The racket from the motorcycle was deafening as it approached. He waited for one more heartbeat, then pivoted around the corner, leading with the submachine gun, every sense tracking where the biker would be as he approached.

The motorcycle was almost on top of him, the biker looking left, anticipating where he expected his victims to be. He was just starting to lower his pistol, clutched in his right hand and pointed at the ceiling, to aim. But the time he saw Bolan and tried to correct, it was too late.

Bolan sighted on the rider's chest and fired a short burst. The dozen or so bullets chopped into the man's rib cage, pulverizing his organs, one round ricocheting up under his helmet to burrow through his jaw and into his brain. It wouldn't have mattered anyway. The cluster of bullets that had mangled his chest, heart and lungs had done more than enough damage to kill him. The brain shot just brought his death ninety seconds faster.

The man fell off his bike, which, unbalanced, wobbled off into crash to the concrete. Again Bolan was moving, jogging back to the SUV and pulling Dae-jung out from underneath it. The Korean lay motionless, and for a heart-stopping moment, Bolan thought a stray round had found him. Then he twitched and a gasping snort escaped from his lips. Saliva burbled at the corner of his mouth as the scientist snored loudly.

He'd passed out!

Shaking his head, Bolan got the scientist up into a fire-man's carry and walked to the next bay. Turning and walking halfway down, he saw the brake lights of a metallic-green SUV flash twice.

"Tell me you just did that, Akira."

"You got it, Striker. I just unlocked your doors. Dump the drunk in the back and hit the road. Your flight out of the city just touched down at Changi. The window's only open for one hour, so you best get going."

Bolan opened the rear passenger door and dumped Dae-jung into the seat, taking a moment to secure him with a lap belt, then got in the driver's seat and pushed the start button. "Assuming nothing else waylays us on the road, we should arrive at the airport with time to spare."

He backed out and headed down the ramp, careful to

avoid the wrecked cycles in the lane. There was a stop bar blocking the exit lane, but as Bolan accelerated toward it, it rose out of his way, and he exited onto Bayfront Avenue. The avenue would lead to Marina Square, and eventually to the East Coast Parkway, one of the main highways circling the city, which would take him to Changi Airport.

Bolan adjusted the driver's seat and started to breath a little easier as he sped up to match traffic. He checked his rearview mirror but didn't see any outward sign of a disturbance—no police cars or hotel security cordoning off the entryway, no riot police storming the place. Except for a nondescript panel delivery van approaching fast with its high beams on, it seemed they had gotten away without a trace.

The van suddenly sped up until it was right on the Toyota's bumper, its high-beam headlights flooding the entire passenger compartment with light. Bolan flipped up the mirror to redirect the beams and moved over to another lane. The van stayed right with him. Seeing only light traffic ahead, Bolan gunned the engine, the SUV leaping forward. Caught by surprise, the van driver tried to catch up, his engine roaring as he pulled alongside Bolan's vehicle. The window in the side door opened, and a man poked out a gun barrel, aiming at him.

The moment he saw the muzzle, Bolan wrenched the Harrier's steering wheel hard left. The SUV slammed into the van, making it veer into another lane. Seeing a semi truck ahead of them, Bolan swerved right, narrowly missing the trailer. He pushed down on the gas pedal, seeing a sign that read Changi Airport: 4 Km.

"Just have to keep this sucker rolling for another couple miles."

"Tell me you haven't attracted more attention." Tokaido's voice was resigned.

Bolan checked his mirror—the van was still on his

tail. "Must be the motorcycle jockeys' backup. It looks big enough to hold two bikes. Hang on, they're coming up again."

The van was creeping up on the driver's side once more. Bolan let it come, even setting the cruise control on the SUV to about eighty miles per hour and resting the loaded MP-9 in his lap. He checked his side mirror, watching the van inch closer to his Toyota. Although traffic on the highway was fairly heavy at this hour, Bolan couldn't wait to find an empty spot to take out his pursuers. The other drivers would just have to take their chances.

"Just try not to attract any police," Tokaido said. "Your current cargo would be very difficult to explain to the local constabulary."

Bolan checked his mirrors again, gauging the distance. "Don't worry, I have every intention of ending this as quickly as possible."

The van surged forward, now only about ten yards away. A shadow appeared in the van's side window again, and that was when Bolan made his move.

Holding the wheel steady with his left hand, he lowered the driver's window, stuck out the MP-9, and emptied the magazine into the van's windshield. The laminated safety glass was tough, but not designed to take that kind of abuse. It shattered into hundreds of tiny nuggets as the burst of fire chopped the heads and chests of the driver and front passenger into pâté.

With no one at the wheel, the van slewed to the left, cutting off a BMW as it careened hard into the concrete divider, sparks flying as its front fender crumpled under the impact. Bolan glanced back in time to see it flip onto its side, skidding down the road toward him. Increasing the gas, Bolan watched the van recede in his rearview mirror as the traffic began to slow and bottleneck behind it.

About a mile later, he reached the turnoff for the airport and took it. "Where am I going, Akira?"

"Follow the signs for T2 Boulevard, and keep bearing right. Your private jet is awaiting you at the second hangar."

Bolan rounded one more turn and saw a sleek Gulfstream G650 jet waiting. "Well, at least I get to ride back in style."

"You can thank the State Department for the ride. Word is they confiscated it from a drug smuggler in Bogotá, and Hal has the pull to use it, no questions asked."

Bolan pulled up next to the hangar and turned off the engine.

Sliding out of the driver's seat, Bolan opened the back passenger door and unbuckled his cargo, who was still snoring loudly. "Slept through the whole thing."

Tossing the unconscious man over his shoulder, Bolan headed for the entry stairs to the jet.

"Good to see you, Mr. Cooper. I trust you had a pleasant time in Singapore?" The pilot grinned.

"What the hell're you doing here, Jack?"

Jack Grimaldi pushed back the pilot's cap on his head and grinned. "Well, Dragon Slayer is undergoing some upgrades to its flight computers, and Able and Phoenix are handling missions that don't need my special talents, so when Hal said they needed someone to extract your ass out of Singapore, and that the someone would be piloting a brand-new Gulfstream, who was I to refuse?"

Bolan grinned at his long-time pilot and good friend's enthusiasm. "Well, let me stow my package and let's get out of here. I'm due a long rest after chasing this guy all over Southeast Asia for the past two weeks, and this flight'll be a good start."

"Aww, and here I thought you and I'd hit the town once you'd wrapped up your business." Grimaldi followed Bolan up the steps, poking the limp Dae-jung. "Anyone I should know?"

"Only if you have a terrible interest in North Korea's nuclear program."

"Nah, I'll leave that to the government types." Grimaldi activated the door controls to seal the door and pressurize the interior as he headed to the cockpit while Bolan secured their passenger. As he sat Dae-jung in a plush, white leather captain's chair, the scientist convulsed once, then hunched over and vomited—all over the carpet and Bolan's shoes.

Staring at the mess, Bolan just shook his head. "Perfect."

4

Binoculars in hand, Park Ranger Sarah Dantlinger scanned the rocky terrain, searching for the slightest movement below as the Bell 206A JetRanger helicopter skimmed over Yellowstone National Park at one thousand feet. Beside her, pilot Mark Azoff kept the chopper straight and level as he perused the lush forest and grassy meadows on their left side.

"Got anything yet?" she asked over the intercom.

"Nope. You're sure they're out here somewhere?"

"That's what ground said—five hikers on a day trip along Specimen Ridge. I just wish we'd had more information from their distress call."

The two park rangers were looking for a family of five that had called in a patchy distress call on a cell phone. Since the call was too garbled to make out exactly what they were saying, headquarters had dispatched Dantlinger and Azoff in the Bell to locate the hikers and assess their situation.

Dantlinger continued scanning the area, her Zeiss binoculars making the parched meadows and forest leap into sharp relief below. She caught a black bear foraging for food to add to its winter bulk, and a fox that was there one moment and gone the next as the chopper's clatter made it dart into the underbrush.

"Wait a minute! I got a trail!" Azoff slewed the Bell around so Dantlinger could get a look at the line of crushed grass that meandered across a field and petered out in some foothills. Following the line with her optics, Dantlinger saw a man waving his shirt over his head about one hundred yards away.

"Got 'em! Can you put it down here?"

"It looks all right from here, but that grass could be hiding a stump, branch, or rock—too dangerous to risk a full touchdown. I'm gonna have to hover and let you off."

"Okay."

Thirty seconds later, Dantlinger opened the door and stepped out onto the landing skid. Holding her flat-brimmed ranger's hat in her hand, the wash from the rotors made her blink against the powerful wind. The ground was a few feet below, and she jumped carefully, ready to tuck and roll if she had to. Fortunately she landed on solid, level ground. Ducking as she sprinted away from the blurred blades spinning overhead, Dantlinger ran to the man, who hadn't come out to meet her, but was waiting at the base of the hill.

"Thanks for coming. Hey, where's he going?" the man asked as Azoff powered the chopper back into the air. He was only a few inches taller than Dantlinger's five-feet-six-inches, with the beginnings of a pot belly. He was inappropriately dressed for the season, in khaki cargo pants, a T-shirt and the plaid, short-sleeved madras shirt he'd used as a signal. Despite the short autumn day, his face was pink from exposure to the sun.

Weekend camper, for sure, she thought as she stared at him. "It's very dangerous to perform a controlled hover that close to the ground. You are the group that called in the distress signal, right? What's the emergency?" she asked while taking in the rest of the family—a sullen teenage girl with purple and black hair who was listening to music on her MP3 player, a pair of twins a few years younger than her who were both watching the helicopter in awe as it did a lazy circle around the area, and the wife, a bottle-blonde in an L.L. Bean windbreaker and designer jeans who was sitting on ground, staring up at Dantlinger with a familiar, expectant expression.

"Oh, there's no emergency here, thank goodness. We're just done for the day and want a ride back to camp before nightfall." The man also stared at her expectantly, as if he was waiting for her to doff her hat and bow to him before saying, "Of course, sir, right this way."

Dantlinger looked over her shoulder to check the position of the Bell as she blew out a patient breath. "Sir, the helicopters in Yellowstone are not a transport service, they are *only* for use in emergency situations."

"So what does that mean?" he asked.

"That means I'm going to radio my partner, he's going to bring the helicopter back down, I'm going to climb in, and he and I are going to fly away. You and your party are welcome to begin hiking back to your campsite. If you hurry, you can make it before nightfall."

"What the hell do you mean by that? Look, girl, you're already here. You might as well take us back with—"

Dantlinger's voice turned frosty as she cut the man off. "First, we are not obligated to do anything for you. No one here is in any immediate physical danger, nor is the weather likely to turn inclement in the next several hours. Second, we cannot take all of you back in the helicopter, as it only seats five, and I'm damn sure not gonna spend a night out here because you people didn't plan your hike properly. Lastly, during the time we would spend transporting you back to your site, a *real* emergency could be happening that we couldn't answer because we're carrying you and your family. Again, I advise you to get your family moving and start following the trail you left back to your campsite."

Dantlinger turned and began heading back to the landing area, waving her arm to signal Azoff to set back down.

"Goddamnit, you can't talk to me that way! I pay your goddamn salaries out here, and I—" Shouting, the man came after her and clapped a meaty hand on her shoulder, intending to spin her.

Dantlinger dropped her shoulder and twisted away, slipping out of his grasp. Her hand dropped to the canister of pepper spray on her belt, but she didn't draw it. "Sir! Do not attempt to grab me again! I suggest you gather your family up and begin hiking back to your campsite."

"You little bitch, you're not gonna walk away from me!" The man lunged forward, hands outstretched to grab her shirt.

Grabbing his arm, Dantlinger stepped to the side and executed a judo flip over her hip. The man somersaulted head over heels and ended up flat on his back, staring up at her and at his arm, which was still held firmly in her grasp. His pink face turned even redder as he gasped for breath after the bone-jarring impact. Dantlinger heard a cry of alarm from the wife and bent over the man.

"Before you even think about filing a lawsuit, keep in mind that I've got six witnesses who will testify that you grabbed me first. Do yourself a favor, get up and get moving." Releasing his arm, she strode off, ignoring the curses and threats of legal action following her.

At the chopper, she opened the door and climbed inside. "Let's go."

"Let me guess—another tourist family who hiked out too far and wanted a lift back?"

"Got it in one."

Azoff's face darkened behind his aviator sunglasses. "Did he try to put his hand on you?"

"He tried but didn't get very far. Don't worry about it. We heading back?"

"Nope. While you were out there parleying with the weekend warriors, we got a real distress call—a hiker took a tumble down a rock face seven miles from here, fractured her ankle and is stuck on a vertical wall."

"Then let's go help someone who really needs it." Casting a stern glance at the family on the ground, Dantlinger shook her head as the Bell rose into the air and headed to their next call.

Ten minutes later, Dantlinger exited the chopper atop a wind-worn cliff where three hikers clustered, waving them down. Carrying climbing rope, carabiners, pitons, a rock hammer and two climbing harnesses, she climbed out and jogged over.

"Hi, I'm Park Ranger Sarah Dantlinger. Where's your other member?"

One of the hikers, a bearded, scruffy-haired man, pointed over the sheer face. He was breathing a bit fast, although his voice was controlled. "She got too close, even though we warned her, and part of the face gave way, making her lose her balance. She slid down and ended up on a ledge about forty feet down. Can you get her out safely?"

"I'm certainly going to try. What's your name?"

"Efraim."

"Okay, Efraim, you're my contact person up here. When I talk to the three of you, I only want you to answer, okay?"

He nodded.

"What's her name?"

"Claire."

"Okay, can you guys stand back, please?" Dantlinger went to the edge of the cliff. "Claire? Claire, can you hear me?"

"Yes!" came a cry from below.

"I'm Park Ranger Sarah Dantlinger. I'm coming down to help you."

"Okay!"

"Are you stable down there? Are you in any danger of falling?"

"No, the ledge is a foot wide at least and pretty sturdy. My ankle hurts something fierce though."

"Okay, I'm tossing a rope down, then I'm going to come to you. Please do not try to climb the rope when you see it."

Dantlinger stepped into her harness, hammered a piton into a sturdy crack at the top of the cliff and tossed the rope over the side. Holding herself steady, she backed up to the cliff edge and lowered herself over until she was standing on the vertical face. Slowly she began rappelling down the wall, using her arms and legs to control her descent. Within two minutes she was at the ledge and carefully stepped onto it.

Claire was a fair-skinned redhead who was sitting with her legs drawn up to her chin. Her eyes seemed clear, and her speech wasn't slurred at all.

"How're you doing?"

"My ankle is killing me, and I'm cold from sitting on this rock, but otherwise I'm okay. Can you get me out of here?"

Dantlinger checked the young woman's ankle, ensuring that it wasn't a compound or other serious fracture that might be made worse by moving her. "That's the plan. Do you think you can put this harness on?"

"Maybe. I might need some help, though."

"All right, let me get my partner set up, and then we'll get you prepped." Sarah got her radio. "Mark, we're gonna have to use a short-haul evacuation. I'll set up the first line with the group topside."

"Affirmative, ready to release on your signal."

Dantlinger clicked off her radio and shouted at the top, "Efraim!"

"Yeah?"

"The helicopter is going to send a line down to you. When you receive it, keep feeding it down to me here, okay?"

"Okay!"

Dantlinger got on her radio. "Mark, we are go."

"Affirmative, releasing line."

A few seconds later, a thin line attached to a beanbag came snaking down the rock face. Meanwhile, Claire had managed to get her harness on.

Dantlinger drew in the small line until she got to the thicker line. Attaching a carabiner to a secure knot, she helped Claire over to it. "Okay, we're both going to attach ourselves to the line, and then Mark, my pilot, is gonna lift us away from the rock face. Our main concern will be to keep from swinging too hard, as that might drive us back into the cliff wall. Don't worry about Mark. He's one of the best. You just hold on to me and keep your eyes on my face. Ready?"

Claire nodded, her lips tight and face white with fear. Dantlinger made sure they were both clipped in securely, then curled one arm around Claire and gave one last command to Azoff. "Go for evac." Letting the radio dangle from its wrist strap, she grabbed the line above her head as they were gently lifted off the ledge. A startled gasp came from Claire, but she maintained her composure well.

Azoff lifted them to the top of the cliff wall and set them down as gently as he would a kitten. Sarah released both her and Claire, examined the young woman's ankle, wrapped it and got her aboard the helicopter. After making sure the others could get back in one piece, she climbed aboard and they took off for the nearest hospital.

NINETY MINUTES LATER, Azoff and Dantlinger climbed out of the helicopter, which was on the pad next to the ranger headquarters at Mammoth Hot Springs. Although they had a clinic there, they'd flown Claire to the hospital in Jackson Hole, just to be safe. They were walking to the building to wrap up paperwork before heading home when head ranger Randy Jermaine ran up to them.

"Hi Sarah, Mark. Great work with that fallen climber. What was the story on the earlier distress call?"

Dantlinger exchanged a knowing glance with Azoff. "Oh, just tourists with a false alarm, that's all."

"Look, I know you guys are supposed to be done for the day, but I got one more quick call for you. After that, you're finished, I promise."

Both rangers eyed their superior warily. "What's the call?" Jermaine was usually a pretty good boss, but sometimes he could go off on people, and a few times a year Darlinger, Azoff, or one of the other rangers would have to intercede to calm down an upset tourist over what was usually a minor infraction. The way he was clasping his hands in front of his belt, Sarah thought this might be one of those times.

"Normally I wouldn't send someone out in the first place, but we just got a call about six campers supposed to be on a weeklong trip at the campsite at DeLacy Creek. This afternoon, one of their parents called and said she couldn't raise any of them on their cells for two days. She talked to other parents as well as friends and says no one's heard from them in at least thirty-six hours. I know cell service is spotty out here at best, but that's a long time for such a large party to be totally out of communication. I'd like you two to drive down there and check on them. I'll even authorize the overtime if needed."

Dantlinger shrugged. "Sure, I can go. Mark, you don't have to if you don't want. Sounds like a simple checkup."

"Thanks, but if I don't, I'll have to go home to the uber-pregnant one, which will not be pleasant." Azoff's wife was in the ninth month of carrying twins, and every day he regaled the crew with hilarious stories about his home life. Just then his cell phone dinged. He took it out and flipped it over, his jaw dropping as he read the text. "Kellie's water just broke. Her mom's taking her to the hospital right now...I gotta go!"

Jermaine nodded and waved Azoff toward his pickup. "Get outta here—and keep us posted!"

After watching Azoff tear across the parking lot to his truck, Jermaine glanced at Dantlinger. "So, do you want any backup?"

"Nah, don't worry about it. Probably some college kids who let their batteries on their cell phones and laptops die."

"I don't know—all I see nowadays are these kids with those damn smartphones and tablets and players and who knows what else running around listening to music while texting one friend and calling another and not paying attention to what's happening around them."

"Yup, sounds like the typical American teenager. Gimme the keys to the Suburban. I'll go take a look and call you from the site."

"It's site A6, toward the back." Jermaine tossed her the set of keys, and Dantlinger walked off just as she spotted the tired, bedraggled family of campers she'd encountered on the ridge earlier pull into camp.

Uh-oh—they aren't camping around here. Might be a good time to slip away in case that blowhard is actually going to file a complaint, Dantlinger thought. Slipping behind the wheel of the five-year old SUV, she pulled out of the lot, glancing back to see the father stomping over to the ranger headquarters. *Oh boy—bet I'll hear about this later.*

But even the possibility of a reprimand couldn't dampen Dantlinger's spirits as she drove down Grand Loop Road toward the campsite in question, about forty-five miles away. Having moved out here from San Diego and the wreckage of a failed marriage and destroyed career, she'd found a new life in the rugged beauty of the park. Even living on half her former salary didn't bother her; it had been surprising to find what she could do without on a daily or weekly basis. She'd given up designer clothes, luxury cars, a palatial home and a six-figure income for a simpler life here in Yellowstone National Park, and hadn't regretted it for a minute. In her third year at the park, she knew most of it like the back of her hand, and loved exploring its nooks and crannies even on her days off.

Jeff would never have understood any of it, she thought, glancing at the beautiful palette of light created as the sun began sinking behind the western mountains. Of course, he would have been too busy fucking any available woman who crossed his path anyway.

The memory of her philandering husband made her stomach clench, and Dantlinger pushed the dark thought away. *He's moved on to ruin someone else's life, not my problem,* she thought.

Traffic was pretty much nonexistent at that time of year, and she made good time on the Loop, the Suburban's tires humming on the pavement as she wound around the twisting, turning road. Eventually she came to the campsite in question and pulled in, but found no sign of anyone. The fire pits were cold and dark, the garbage barrels were empty, and there were no footprints or tent peg holes anywhere. However, Dantlinger noticed tire tracks leading from the site farther into the woods.

She called in as she got back into the Suburban. "Randy? I'm at the campsite. There's no one here. Tire tracks lead north, however, so I'm going to drive a bit farther in, see if they might have made a gypsy site somewhere."

"Affirmative. Um, Sarah. That false alarm you mentioned earlier—was there anything else you wanted to tell me about it?"

Dantlinger sighed, but too quietly for Jermaine to hear before she replied. "When I was explaining that the helicopter was for emergencies to a bunch of tourists who wanted a ride back to their campsite, the father of the group grew hostile and verbally abusive. He put his hand on my shoulder in an confrontational way. I evaded it, then he lunged at me, which forced me to physically subdue him."

"Did you escalate the confrontation in any way?"

"You mean use my baton or pepper spray? No, it wasn't necessary."

"Well, that's not how he's telling it. He says you were verbally abusive and attacked him when he tried to ask for help. I'm gonna need you to come back and give me a full report on this right away."

"I'll be there ASAP, Randy, but I'm gonna take a quick look for those kids first."

"Sarah, this is import—" Her boss's words were cut off by Dantlinger's turning her radio off.

"Oops, I think we got some interference. Guess I'll have to get back to you on that." She pulled out of the campsite and drove deeper into the forest, following an old mining road that had almost been completely swallowed by the forest over the decades. On the way she reviewed the encounter and realized that she might be in a bit more trouble than she'd thought. It was his word against hers, but if his family backed up his version of the story, Azoff's account as a witness while several hundred feet away and flying a helicopter to boot might not count for a lot. The first tickle of fear surfaced in her stomach as she thought about the possibility of getting suspended, maybe even fired over this.

Dantlinger took a deep breath and steeled her gaze straight ahead. *You've made it through a lot worse than this,* she thought, *so you can survive dealing with some blustering blowhard, too.*

She continued down the narrow road until she came to a clearing. Pulling off to the side, she got out, took a four-cell Maglite from the truck seat beside her and walked around the area, shining the light everywhere.

Almost immediately she found evidence that someone had been here. There were tire tracks in the dirt, and several sets of footprints going all over. A crude fire ring had been constructed out of rocks, with the large pile of fairly new ashes inside indicating that a large fire had been built in the past few days.

Dantlinger scanned the rapidly darkening tree line, looking for evidence of anything unusual, like a bear wandering into the camp looking for food, perhaps. Except for the signs of people, the empty clearing was eerily silent.

She returned her light and her attention to the ring of stones around the campfire. They looked odd, like they'd been disturbed and hastily shoved back into a rough approximation of where they'd originally been. As she played her light slowly over the ashes, a glint caught her eye. Squatting, Sarah picked up the item that had got her attention.

A dusty 9 mm shell casing rested in her hand. She quickly poked through the rest of the fire's remains, but came up with nothing else out of the ordinary. Several of the rocks, however, had dark stains on them.

Dantlinger straightened and looked around again,

unease making her shoulder blades tingle. Starting from the fire, she began walking in a widening spiral, constantly expanding the circle she had started from the center point of the fire pit. Although most of the footprints around the fire looked to be from sneakers, she found two sets of what appeared to be combat boots that seemed to come from the nearby forest.

Something happened here—something bad, she thought. Slipping the bullet casing into her pocket, she grabbed several of the stained rocks, loaded them into the back of the Suburban, got in, turned it, and headed back to the headquarters, switching on her radio on the way.

"Sarah, where the hell have you been—?"

"Randy, this isn't the time. I've been to the DeLacy Creek campsite, and I think something bad happened there. I'm coming back right away."

"Wait, what? What are you talking—"

Dantlinger turned the volume down on her radio as she pressed the gas pedal, making the big SUV shake and surge forward down the deserted road.

5

As he drove on Highway 287 through the mountains north of Norris, Montana, Bolan enjoyed an almost priceless moment of pure relaxation.

The weather in the Rockies on this mid-October afternoon was clear and crisp, the round sun high in the sapphire-blue sky, allowing him to take in the stark yet beautiful countryside, rolling hills covered with swaths of timothy grass parched brown over summer giving way to grass-covered foothills, with those topped by rugged rocky peaks soaring thousands of feet into the air.

Bolan's Cadillac Escalade purred down the smooth, empty road, its Vortec V8 engine providing more than enough power to get him to his destination. For the moment, he was content to simply drive, letting his ever-present war on terror and those who would threaten liberty around the world take a back seat for a while.

While he was always the consummate warrior, Bolan also realized that even the finest soldier's edge could become dull after too many missions. Living on the edge 24/7 fatigued the strongest of men, with constant alertness against enemies wearing down reflexes and even worse, intelligence. Bolan's self-declared war was never-ending, but he was also smart enough to know he was no good to anyone if he got killed because he'd pushed even his abilities too far.

After his whirlwind trip zigzagging around Southeast Asia, Bolan had loaded up the SUV and taken off, driving two thousand miles in thirty-six hours. Rather than exhausting him, the solo road trip had cleared his mind while reconnecting him to the land he loved. From crossing the Appalachians and the Mississippi River to heading through the seemingly endless plains of the nation's former breadbasket to the plateaus and foothills of the western states before the Rockies, Bolan had enjoyed it all. He'd stopped at truck stops and small-town cafés, relishing the anonymity of being just another faceless traveler among hundreds of men and women on the road.

His pulse quickened as he neared the end of his journey, and the second leg he was about to embark on. Bolan had reserved a secluded campsite in Yellowstone, and was looking forward to several days of camping, hiking and most of all, solitude. While he had nothing against people in general, sometimes a man just wanted to get back to nature and spend some time there with only his thoughts for company.

Cresting a long, gradual hill, Bolan came upon the small town of Norris. Consisting of about a dozen small businesses and roughly twice as many houses scattered along the highway, its primary claim to fame rested on two things—the Museum of the National Park Ranger, housed in a single-story log building that Bolan was sure was full of history on the rangers, but which he had no interest in seeing, and the nearby hot springs. Instead, he turned into the parking lot of a combination gas and grocery store at the intersection of Highway 84 and 287. After filling his tank, he went inside and stocked up on enough food to last the entire trip.

The cashier was a burly, old man with tufts of thinning, white hair poking out from under a John Deere gimme cap above a seamed face. One of his arms ended in a steel claw, but he handled it like he'd been born with it, ringing Bolan's purchases up and bagging them without a pause. "Comin' or goin'?"

"Coming. Spending a few days upcountry." Bolan pointed vaguely at the mountains in the distance to the east, the opposite direction of where he was ultimately headed.

"Good time to be here—less tourists and traffic this time of year."

Bolan picked up his bag. "I thought towns like this depended on the trade."

The corner of the old man's mouth crooked up in what might have been a smile. "Oh, don't get me wrong. We like seein' 'em come in, but we also like seein' 'em head back out, as well."

Smiling at the man's blunt honesty, Bolan shifted his groceries to the crook of his arm. "Well, then, before I do the same, did you happen to hear the latest weather report?"

"Yup. Supposed to be clear and bright the next few days, highs in the low thirties, lows in the teens. Course, haven't had our first real snow yet, and the higher you go, the more chance you have of it comin' down, so if your headin' into the mountains, you best be prepared for anything."

"Thanks for the advice. I think I'm more than prepared for whatever the mountains can dish out. Take care."

"You, too." The man tipped his cap with his hook as Bolan walked outside. The soldier breathed in the crisp mountain air and looked around once more. Nothing but peace and silence in every direction.

Yeah, I'm definitely gonna enjoy my time here, he thought as he set the bag in the back, got into the driver's seat and pulled out onto Sterling Road, heading due west.

TEN MINUTES LATER, Bolan pulled up into the driveway of the information station and bookstore outside the town of Madison as the sun was beginning to sink below the horizon. He introduced himself under his Matt Cooper alias at the main building, a long, low, log structure, complete with stone fireplace and a small supply store.

There were only a couple people in the building besides the attendant. After giving the pair—a gray-bearded man sporting a ponytail and an intense-looking woman in black cargo pants and short blond hair—a cursory glance, Bolan bought some extra batteries.

"To get to the campsite at Scaup Creek, I just keep going down the main road, correct?" he asked.

The cashier was a blond, crew-cut teen with a half-dozen earrings in his left ear. "Yup, just follow the Loop for another twenty-two miles. The campsite will be marked by signs on your left. Enjoy your stay."

"Thanks." Bolan headed out to his Escalade.

Only after he had driven off did the couple walk outside, the woman dialing a number on her cell phone. When the call went through, she said. "We may have a problem at A5. Lone camper, male, Caucasian, about six-three, two hundred pounds, black hair, heading right for the area. Suggest sending the team to check him out."

"Will evaluate and take all appropriate measures," the voice on the other end said. "Return to base camp and prepare for arrival of final package."

"Affirmative." She flipped the cell phone closed and nodded to her companion. Getting into their Jeep Cherokee, she started the engine and drove off, following the same road Bolan had taken.

6

Truly this is a promised land, Arkady Novikov thought as he lowered the encrypted cell phone and stared out at the hauntingly beautiful landscape around him. Back home he would compare the Rocky Mountains with the majesty of the Ural Mountains, the range that bisected Western Russia, and be hard-pressed to declare which one was more breathtaking.

Of course, these days, he thought, it would probably be the Rockies, which have not suffered the depredations of its nation's citizens for many years. His own homeland had not been so lucky. Thousands of square miles in the Southern Urals had been polluted for decades by the plutonium-producing factory Mayak, located in Chelyabinsk-65, Ozyorsk. Built in 1948, the facility had dumped raw radioactive waste into the Techa River and Lake Karachay for the first ten years of operation. Although a decade-long effort had been started to contain the radiation in the lake, it still contained more millirems than a human should be exposed to in a year. In 1957, a storage tank explosion had contaminated thousands more miles of countryside. Even today, although some of its reactors had been shut down, the facility still produced plutonium.

Of course, incidents of birth defects, cancer and other

health issues had skyrocketed, plaguing the population of the area throughout the following generations. Novikov's parents had left the area when he was an infant and settled closer to Moscow, but the poison they had lived in had claimed both before their time, his mother from leukemia, his father from cancer, invisible tendrils of radioactivity that had reached across thousands of miles from their blighted home and claimed their lives.

And here I stand, he thought, *in this vast, unspoiled wilderness, awaiting the method of the world's destruction—which uses that same polluting, destroying element that destroyed my home and family. The irony is rich indeed.*

Novikov was sixty miles away from Yellowstone National Park, standing on a completely deserted, windswept plain in southern Montana, awaiting the people whom he had spent two years courting, and the object that he'd purchased for several hundred thousand dollars.

If only they knew what we're planning to do with the device, he thought. *I do not think they would be so eager to complete this transaction.* The thought made him smile. Everything they were doing was transitory—one single point on a timelines that spanned millennia—and had been for years, ever since he had come up with the plan in one brilliant insight several years ago. Since then, every waking instant had been channeled toward the next two days, when he and a group of like-minded individuals would change the world forever.

The highway he stood next to was a black strip bisecting the featureless plains all around him. In the half hour he had stood there, he hadn't seen another human or vehicle. But finally Novikov saw a dot appear on the horizon from the west. He gave it five minutes to approach closer before he activated the walkie-talkie feature on his cell phone.

"This is Alpha. They are coming. Maintain your positions. No one is to act unless I give the signal."

His words might have been unheeded except for four distinctly audible clicks from the cell phone's speaker. Novikov replaced the phone in his coat pocket and waited, the prairie wind ruffling his thinning brown hair.

A few more minutes passed. The vehicle on the horizon solidified into a panel truck, its sides bearing a garish advertisement for a children's birthday party company, featuring a vaguely sinister clown who appeared to be reaching out for the viewer, the expression on his painted face a cross between a smile and a leer. There were two men in the front of the truck, and Novikov had no doubt that there were at least two more in the cargo compartment.

His hands remained in his pockets.

The truck pulled to a stop several yards behind his van. For a moment the men in the truck watched Novikov watch them. His cell phone trilled. The Russian pulled it out and answered.

"You came alone?" a gruff voice asked.

Novikov slowly looked to the left and the right. "There is no one else around that I can see."

"Once we hang up, you will keep the phone in your hand and keep both hands in plain sight at all times. You will walk to the back of the truck, where you will be searched thoroughly. If you are carrying any sort of listening device or weapon, the meeting will end. Do you understand?"

"I have followed the rules as you have stated them."

"The payment is in the bags?"

Novikov looked down at his feet, where two large, black, canvas bags sat on the ground in front of him. "That is correct."

"Put your forearms through the carrying straps and bring the bags to the rear of the truck. The bags will also be searched, and several bills tested. If anything unusual is found, the meeting will end. Do you understand?"

"Yes. You are aware that I will need to see the device before handing over payment?"

"You will once we have verified that the payment is genuine."

Novikov's ice-cold nerves twitched a bit at this—not from fear, for he had conquered that primitive reaction years ago—but from the thought that they might betray and kill him, or that the device he was buying would turn out to be a fake and compromise the entire mission. He quickly banished the thought; the selling party had been able to prove that they possessed what he had been looking for at every step of the negotiations, and there was no reason to think they would try anything at this point. But even so, he was on high alert as he followed the instructions. The bags were heavy on his arms—four million dollars in one-hundred-dollar bills was a lot of paper.

When he turned the rear corner of the truck, he was met with a second pair of men, both wearing ski masks. The farthest one, about seven feet away, held an Uzi submachine gun in his hands. The nearer one walked over to him, holding some kind of scanning device.

Set the bags down and hold your arms straight out from your sides."

Novikov did so, waiting silently as the man scanned the bags first, then his torso and limbs, first with one device, then with another. The second device beeped slightly as it passed over his upper chest. The closer man glared at Novikov, while the farther man tightened his grip on the Uzi.

Novikov remained calm. "It must be picking up the stylus in my shirt pocket. I use it on my smartphone."

Making sure the Uzi-wielding man had a clear line of fire, the first man unzipped Novikov's jacket and examined his shirt pocket. There, just as he had told him, was a small metal stylus with a plastic tip, useful for tapping on a phone screen, and not much else.

With a nod, the man then put his metal detector away and patted Novikov down. He was very thorough in this as well, leading Novikov to believe this man had training in law enforcement from somewhere. He endured it stoically.

At last, the man straightened and opened the metal door to the back of the truck. "Pick up the bags and place them inside the cargo bay, then come inside."

Novikov grabbed the side of the truck and stepped up, watching how the men moved as he entered the cargo area. They were either well trained or they had worked together before, as the talking man was careful not to get too close to or block the gun-wielding man's field of fire.

The setting sun threw its dying rays on an eight-foot-long, three-foot-wide, two-foot-high metal box, the only thing in the bed. Novikov's breath quickened as he saw it, but his expression remained calm. "I am going to remove a small radiation detector from my pocket."

The two men exchanged glances. "All right—slowly."

Novikov took out a small device on his key chain, held it near the box and turned it on. The moment he did, the device emitted a loud series of short beeps and a red light on it flashed quickly. It was radioactive. He turned to the men. "I will need to see it with my own eyes."

"Go ahead." The unarmed one was kneeling beside one of the bags, testing sample bills with a counterfeit-detecting marker. The other one still held the Uzi at the ready. Novikov smiled in the twilight. Even if the meeting went off without a hitch, at most they would only have about a week to spend their payment once Novikov's plan was executed.

The shadows were growing inside the truck, and Novikov took out a small headlight, put it on his forehead and turned it on. The men didn't comment on that. He flipped open the six catches on the box and lifted the lid. If seeing the box had made him breathe faster, what he saw inside almost took his breath away.

Resting on crude wooden supports, the lone item inside was a cone of smooth, milled, cream-white steel. The Russian found the maintenance access hatch and popped it open, revealing the guts of the nuclear warhead that was supposed to be inside a RS-12M Topol Intercontinental Ballistic Missile about ten thousand miles away. The 550-kiloton nuclear warhead inside should be more than enough to accomplish what he wanted to do. He quickly checked the internal workings against the plans he had memorized. Everything seemed to be in order, including a new battery to power the detonation system. Novikov wasn't taking any chances—he'd brought his own as well. *It is almost within my grasp,* he thought. Closing the maintenance hatch and the cover, he stood, drawing the stylus from his pocket and concealing it in his hand as he turned back to the two men.

"I trust that the payment is satisfactory?"

"Yup, it's all here. Don't know how you tree huggers came up with all this green, but we're set."

"Good. Then I will bring my truck around and off-load my package." Novikov began moving toward the back of the truck when he heard a familiar sound—the ratchet of a cocking lever being pulled back and released. He stopped where he was—approximately three steps closer to the gunman, which would make all the difference in the next few seconds—and slowly raised his hands, fingers still curled around the stylus in his right.

"I'm afraid that's not gonna happen. You see, we got two more parties willing to pay big bucks for this warhead, so, unfortunately, we can't sell it to you. But we are gonna keep your money, and you'll end up buried somewhere out

here on the lone prairie." The two men smiled at their supposed wit.

Novikov did as well, first chuckling, then laughing
out loud. The two men exchanged confused glances as he
roared with mirth. When the gunman took his eyes off the
Russian to check with the second man about what to do,
Novikov moved.

Lunging at the gunman, he stabbed the tip of the metal
stylus—razor-sharp once he had discarded the fake plastic
tip—into the left side of the man's neck, puncturing the ca-
rotid artery. With his left hand, he grabbed the stock of the
Uzi and turned it so it was facing the second man, who was
trying to draw a pistol from inside his coat. Already dying,
the gunman squeezed the trigger of his submachine gun,
the thirty rounds in the magazine almost cutting his partner in two. The sound of the Uzi going off in the enclosed
space, even with one end open to the outside, pounded in
Novikov's ears.

He pushed the dying man away and hit his smartphone's
walkie-talkie feature, giving it two clicks as he ran to the
front of the cargo bay. The truck doors slammed, and he
heard running footsteps approach the back of the truck,
then stop.

"Stevie?" a voice asked. It was followed by two rifle
reports, one almost right after the other, the sounds rolling
across the barren prairie. Two pairs of large holes appeared
in the both sides of the truck walls. Novikov waited a few
seconds, then heard four squelch noises on his smartphone.
He walked back to the edge of the truck, passing the body
of the gunman, twitching as he lay in a growing pool of
his own blood, and jumped down, then went around the
corner.

The driver lay sprawled on the road, his upper chest
blown apart by the huge bullet that had blasted its way
through him. Novikov patted his pockets for the keys

before going to the other side of the truck and seeing the passenger on the ground as well, his head cored by a similar bullet.

Novikov got on his cell phone. "The package is secure. Come in for transfer and cleanup."

Going back to his SUV, he pulled it around to the back of the panel truck. Getting out two heavy-duty garbage bags, he covered the upper body of the driver and the head of the passenger's body, careful not to get any blood on himself.

By the time he was through, he had been joined by four other people. They were all dressed in plain camouflage fatigues from head to toe, complete with face masks and stalks of grass they'd put on their caps to break up their profiles. Two carried smoking .50-caliber rifles, each with a long sound suppressor in the other hand. Both immediately began breaking down their guns. The other two grabbed the bodies and threw them in the back of the truck while Novikov maneuvered his SUV so that its back was facing the cargo bay.

"We good?" one of the men asked.

"Yes." Novikov climbed back into the cargo bed. "Let's move the package."

The four men joined him, and together they hauled the metal box into the SUV.

"What about the money?" another asked.

"We stick to the plan—it gets destroyed with the truck." Novikov closed the SUV's back doors, making sure they were secure. He got an improvised incendiary device, consisting of a detonator and a two-gallon jug filled with equal parts liquid soap and kerosene, and handed it to one of the men. "Team One, drive the truck to the disposal site and clean it thoroughly, then join us at ground zero as soon as possible."

"Yes, Alpha." The two men closed the door, ran to the front of the truck, got in and drove away.

"Team Two—" Novikov was interrupted by his cell phone vibrating. He answered. "Yes?"

"Our insert zone is still compromised, Alpha. The man described earlier is there, setting up his campsite. Instructions?"

"Team Two will be there within two hours. We'll handle him after nightfall." He turned off his phone and addressed the two men. "We have one more loose end to wrap up. Come on."

7

Sitting on a thick, round chunk of log near his crackling fire, Bolan swallowed his last bite of steak as he surveyed his campsite and smiled with satisfaction.

Upon arrival, he'd raised his tent, cleaned and checked his fire pit, and stocked plenty of deadwood for the next couple days. Next he'd turned his attention to dinner—pan-fried steak and potatoes—cooking over the open flame. In a hurry to get here, he hadn't stopped for anything since breakfast, and as he ate his meal, he understood why.

In his never-ending war, Bolan knew to take any moment of respite whenever he could. This was one of those times—he felt like he was a part of the serene, silent calm around him. Already too chilly for mosquitoes, the night was illuminated only by Bolan's fire and the huge, yellow-white harvest moon that hung low on the horizon. Out here, he could almost forget what he did every day, leaving behind—even if just for a few days—the carnage that he both encountered and caused in his fight against Animal Man.

Bolan would never trade the burden he had taken on with anyone. In an ever-more partisan world, with organizations and groups and countries willing to go to absurd lengths to protect themselves or advance their own beliefs over everyone else, someone had to cut through all the red tape and bureaucratic crap to get the job done, whatever it may entail.

For Bolan, it was simple: some folks needed killing. They didn't need a trial or jail time, or any attempts at rehabilitation. They simply needed to be found and a bullet put into their brain, period. It was the best way to ensure that their poison and hate died with them. For crime syndicates and terrorist organizations, it was the same methodology: identify the leader or leaders and kill them. With the head gone, the body often died soon afterward.

It was a simple, straightforward operating procedure that worked more often than not. However, international terrorism was a many-headed hydra; for every head Bolan chopped off, two more sprang up to take its place. Organized crime was the same. Bolan had once said he could go anywhere in the civilized world and find a crime occurring within one hundred feet of the airport. Wherever there was a profit to be made, whether it be from drugs, slavery, women, or weapons, there would be someone around to collect it. Neither outcome was one that Bolan was willing to put up with. Every decent, hard-working citizen of the world—whether he or she was a blue-collar construction worker in Jersey trying to keep a family clothed, housed and fed, or a tribesman in Ghana trying to get a well dug for his village—deserved better.

However, one couldn't simply just charge headlong into the fray, blasting every terrorist or criminal in sight—that would only lead to paranoia and madness. Bolan had spent years stacking the odds in his favor, from assembling his trusted crew at Stony Man Farm to establishing contacts around the world whenever possible. It was a system that had worked well for years, and barring catastrophe, should continue to do so for many more.

But on this night, Bolan was free to relax, look up at the

stars and let the war against evil soldier on without him for a few days. Finishing his potatoes, he washed his pan, plate and silverware in bottled water, then went to the SUV to get out his sleeping bag. As he rummaged around in the cargo area, he noticed the glare of headlights as two other vehicles drove through the campsite.

Looks like I'm not the only one interested in camping this time of year, he thought. Hauling his bag over to the tent, he went inside and laid it out, setting up his portable lantern as well. He planned to catch up on his reading by perusing a new translation of Sun Tzu's *The Art of War.* Tossing the copy of the book on his bag, he ducked back out to begin banking the fire and turn in for the night.

However, when Bolan straightened, he saw three people on the edge of his site. All male, they were dressed in combinations of camouflage and civilian clothing, but all wore forest camo pants. He didn't see any obvious weapons on them, but his warrior's senses twitched at how quietly they had approached—rather like he would have if he was coming into a camp where he thought the inhabitants might be friend or foe.

Bolan's gaze flicked sideways toward the SUV. He'd brought light arms with him, all registered and legal, but they were still packed in the Caddy, as he hadn't expected to need them immediately. He smiled and held up a hand. "Evening. You folks need something?"

The three glanced at one another before the lead man, a balding, professor-looking type in horn-rimmed glasses and a ponytail, nodded back. "Nope, just thought we were gonna be the only ones around here and decided to come down and say hello."

Bolan smiled. "Well, I'll be here for the next few days, but don't worry. I'm the quiet type. Believe me, I'm the last person who'll bother you."

The three men had fanned out, one each on Bolan's left

and right, and the man wearing the glasses standing directly in front of him. "Nice equipment. This your first time out here?"

"Nope, I've been coming here off and on few years now. How about you?"

"This is my first time in Yellowstone. Ought to be quite a blast, I must say." The others thought the man's comment was funny for some reason, for they both chuckled.

"Yeah, the geysers in the area are quite a sight. Be sure to make plenty of time to see them. Some of them can be a bit of a hike to get to."

The man with the glasses nodded, the flames from Bolan's fire reflecting in his lenses and adding a bit of a heated glow to his face. "Oh yes, we're expecting a huge eruption, unlike anything anyone's ever seen before around here. It'll definitely get some attention."

Again that strange chuckle from the other two, like the three of them were sharing a private joke. "But where are my manners?" the speaker said. "Brian Borsythe." He stepped forward and extended a hand.

Bolan took it and shook once. "Matt Cooper."

"What line of work are you in, Matt?"

"I work with the U.S. State Department." Bolan had kept his cover intact, figuring it couldn't hurt to have the mantle of the government on his side for a few more days.

The reaction from his visitors wasn't what he expected, however. Instead of acceptance or being impressed, the three exchanged dark, worried glances before Borsythe forced a smile onto his face. "Taking a break from all that paper pushing, right?"

"Exactly. Just out here for some R and R." Bolan felt that warning twinge again and turned toward his vehicle. "If you guys'll excuse me, I've got a busy day ahead, so I'm gonna turn in. Perhaps I'll see you around the park tomorrow."

Neither Borsythe nor his two compatriots moved. "I'm afraid we can't let you do that, Matt." He sounded completely calm and matter-of-fact.

Bolan took a step toward his SUV—and the man in his path. "I wouldn't advise trying to stop me."

The man did anyway, bringing up his knee in an attempt to nail Bolan in the groin. But the Executioner had seen the move coming from a mile away and twisted at the waist, his thigh blocking the attack. The man cocked his fist back, but Bolan struck first, slamming his forehead into the bridge of the man's nose. There was a sharp *crack* of breaking bone, and the man staggered back, clutching his face.

Aware the other two were coming at him, Bolan turned to face them, intending to subdue the man in the glasses first, then his partner. But both men seemed content to stay far enough apart that he had to divide his attention between the two, and just stand there.

"What the hell do you—" That was when Bolan felt stars explode in his head, and everything went black for a few seconds. He felt rough hands grab him, and his feet were swept out from under him, sending him crashing to the ground.

"Hold that motherfucker! I wanna piece of him!" Bolan's vision had just started to return when he was rocked by a hard punch to his jaw. "Fuckhead broke my nose!"

Bolan took a couple more shots to the head from the guy before he was hauled off. "Stop, stop it, Tau. We need this guy alive for a few more minutes. Omega, Psi, hold him. Get his boots off. We don't need him rabbiting into the trees."

Bolan felt his arms being wrenched and held behind his back. His legs were pinned to the ground as one hiking boot was removed, then the other. All the while his mind raced, trying to figure out who these guys were, where they had come from? Did someone follow him there?

Bolan felt a hand on his hair and his head was yanked back. He opened his eyes to see Borsythe in front of him, that same, strangely placid expression on his face, as if he was about to deliver a lecture to a group of students instead of commanding thugs who were about to beat and kill a man. Next to him were two other men, both clad entirely in camouflage, including face masks, and armed with HK MP-5 submachine guns.

Bolan just stared at the group, trying to make sense of them.

Borsythe shook his head. "I'm sorry about this, Matt, but we need to know if you're really here on vacation, or on more official business. Now, if you tell us what we want to know quickly, then we'll let you go, and no hard feelings. If you don't—" Borsythe's gaze flicked to the fire beside the group. "I'm afraid we'll have to resort to faster methods of getting the truth out of you. So, what's it gonna be?"

Bolan sucked air into his lungs, gasping loudly as he stalled for time. He already knew these guys weren't going to let him walk out of there no matter what he told them. The only option left for him was to escape. "I already... told you the truth...work for the State Department...foreign relations...I'm just here...on a goddamn vacation!"

"So, as far as you know, the United States government is not observing this national park or the surrounding area."

"Look, pal, even if they were, I wouldn't know about it." *Although once I get out of this I'm damn sure gonna find out if anyone is,* he thought. For the moment, however, it would be best to stick to his cover—a frightened government employee. "I deal with things outside the United States—Europe, Asia, stuff like that. I don't have any idea if this area is of interest to any law-enforcement organization."

"Fuck this, Beta, he's lying! Let me work on him for a few minutes. By the time I'm done, he'll be telling us if he wears women's underwear."

"All right, Tau, you've got two minutes, then we'll see what kind of answers we get. Get him on his feet."

Bolan felt his shoulders protest as he was hauled up, but he couldn't see anything, because the moment he was on his feet, the man they called Tau—the one who's nose he'd broken—stepped up and buried his fist in Bolan's stomach. He'd been ready for it and had tightened his muscles against the blow, but it still rocked him hard. The food he'd just eaten roiled in his belly, and he made a conscious effort to keep it down, knowing that if he was going to survive, that he'd need all the energy he could muster.

"Tough guy, huh? We'll see about that." Tau rocked him with a left-right combination that snapped his head back. Bolan tasted blood and was beginning to see red, as well.

"You're pretty tough...when two guys are holding my arms."

"You think I can't take you, asshole? All right, let him go."

The man holding Bolan's right arm spoke. "Tau, I don't think—"

"Just shut up and do it!"

Watching the rest of the group, Bolan noticed the two submachine gun-wielding guys take up positions so they could cover the entire group with their guns. They're either pros, or they've been trained well by somebody, he thought.

"Beta?" the holder asked.

Their leader nodded. "Make it quick, Tau."

The two men released Bolan's arms and stepped aside, but not before the Executioner noticed one of them carrying an HK MP-5 K, the little brother of the larger automatic weapons the other two men carried, but no less dangerous, slung around his back. Returning his gaze to his opponent, Bolan raised his fists. "All right, try that again, you son of a bitch!"

He hadn't even finished his taunt when Tau blurred into action, whipping his leg around in a spinning kick to Bolan's jaw. Although he was ready for it, and had planned to roll with the kick to lessen the impact, Tau's speed still surprised him.

Reeling from the kick to his face, Bolan's vision blurred as he sprawled in the dirt. His jaw ached, and for a moment he thought the blow might have been broken it, but a quick wiggle confirmed it was intact, although it hurt like hell.

Even half-stunned from the blow, his mind worked with its usual clarity, taking in the data he needed to get out of this situation alive. Three of his attackers were loosely ringed around him, all standing within a yard. The other two had established a loose perimeter on the outskirts of his campsite, weapons at the ready. All were pros, with some kind of previous military experience, or extensive militia training—he could tell by the ways they moved, communicated, and worked on him—all done with the minimal amount of effort to achieve the maximum result. Well, all of them except for Tau.

Even sprawled on the ground, Bolan was working, too. Although unarmed and barefoot, they'd made a critical mistake—they'd left his hands free. He dug his fingers into the dirt, searching for a rock or stick he could use as a weapon. His only concern was that they might do some physical damage to ensure he couldn't walk, like cut a hamstring or shoot out a kneecap.

Bolan spit blood into the dirt. "Look, I don't know what else I can tell you. I'm not here on any secret mission, and I don't know anyone who is."

The man who'd kicked him stretched out a boot and pushed the tip into his jaw, levering his face up so he could see Bolan's injuries in the firelight. "Just as I thought—a fuckin' pussy."

Bolan pushed himself so that he was sitting up. His eyes darted back and forth, simulating fear while in reality evaluating the landscape, plotting his escape route. He just needed a few seconds for a distraction…

"I've told you everything I know. Just let me go and I won't tell anyone I saw you, I swear!"

Tau shook his head. "He doesn't know shit. We better finish this. Alpha's waiting, and we need to stay on schedule."

"Just another camper who got lost in the woods—and never came out again." The man on Bolan's right had been threading a sound suppressor onto a SIG-Sauer P-229 pistol, and presently pulled the slide back to chamber a round. The others stepped back to give the man room to work. Bolan's muscles tensed in anticipation of the coming bullet.

The gunman stepped forward to aim the weapon at his prone target. "Wrong place, wrong time, Mr. Cooper—"

Bolan threw the handful of dirt he'd grabbed into the man's face, making him rear backward, clawing at his eyes. The moment the earth left his hand, the soldier lunged up, grabbing the pistol with his left hand and shoving it away so the muzzle pointed into the air. The pistol coughed a round into the night as its surprised owner squeezed the trigger.

That wasn't the prize Bolan was going for. His right hand reached around the back of the man to go for the deadlier weapon—his slung HK MP-5 K, which had been readied to shoot, then left on full-auto with a round in the chamber.

"Kill him!" The rest of the group burst into action, scattering from the two struggling men. Bolan triggered the subgun, stitching the man standing farthest away with several rounds as he was drawing a bead on the fighters. The dead gunner pitched forward, his own HK spitting bullets into the ground.

Bolan kept firing, keeping the others' heads down while he tried to subdue his opponent. His would-be assassin had gone for his pistol, locking both hands on it and trying to lever it down for a shot at Bolan's face. The Executioner saved him the trouble. Pulling the stubby German gun out to the farthest reach of its sling, he triggered a short burst through his opponent's chest. The 9 mm manglers shattered ribs and pulped his heart, dropping the man in his tracks.

Bolan went down with him, pulling the HK off the body and snatching up the SIG in his other hand. He sprayed gunshots all around, relying on instinct and his memory of where the other shooters were to keep their heads down— and hopefully put a bullet or two into one of them.

"Somebody shoot that son of a bitch!"

Return fire was coming at him, and Bolan knew he'd lose a protracted firefight. Triggering a few last shots from the SIG and the HK, he broke for the nearest clump of woods about ten yards away. Bullets kicked up clods of dirt and splintered tree bark and limbs around him. He felt something punch him in the lower back, along the left side, and knew he'd taken a bullet. Adrenaline reduced the pain to a faraway ache, but he'd pay for that later. His feet were quickly becoming cut and bruised by his flight over the rough terrain, but better sore and bloody soles than certain death.

The sound of rushing water caught his attention and Bolan veered toward it, hoping to use the water to cover his tracks or maybe even quick transportation out of the area and back to civilization. Shouts and the sounds of men running through the forest pushed him to move even faster.

The water noise grew louder, and Bolan pushed through a cluster of Douglas firs to see a fast-moving mountain stream flowing by him. It had carved its way through the land over thousands of years, and was presently at the bottom of a ravine. He looked upstream, only to see the stream head deeper into the forest. Fully prepared and armed, he could have done it, but in his current predicament it would only prolong the chase. Downstream was his best option.

The bullet from behind grazed Bolan's head just enough to make him lose his balance and tumble down the incline into the flowing water. The submachine gun flew from his grasp on the way, and the shock of hitting the icy cold flowage made him drop the SIG-Sauer, the pistol disappearing into the black water. It was followed by Bolan himself a second later, who plunged into the swift current and was quickly swept downstream.

8

Still a bit groggy from the beating and stunned from the bullet almost taking him out, Bolan was shocked back to awareness by the icy cold water of the stream. He heard shouts and calls in the distance, and knew his pursuers were still after him. Light shone on the surface of the water, and Bolan ducked under as it played in his direction. The stream wasn't flowing fast enough for him to outrun his hunters. He needed to find a place to hide.

He swam for the far shore, staying underwater until his lungs ached for air. When his hand encountered branches and mud, he followed the escaping bubbles from his lips and turned himself so he was floating faceup. Only then did he relax enough to bring his nose and mouth to the surface of the water for a quick gulp of air.

He heard men calling to one another in the distance, then they suddenly grew quiet. Bolan didn't think they'd left, though. He'd noticed the walkie-talkie each man had clipped to his belt. Most likely they had gone to silent communication to hunt more effectively.

Bolan began pulling himself along the bank, searching for an undercut or submerged tree stump or log he could use as cover. There were no trees nearby, but about ten yards away his questing hand pushed through a carpet of grass roots to find a small space behind them, perhaps a yard square. Ducking underneath the water, he squeezed in behind it, the grassy curtain thick enough to block the moonlight from outside. Finally out of the water enough to breathe, he sucked in a deep gulp of air and clenched his teeth together to keep them from chattering. Although the bone-chilling water would help stop his bleeding by restricting the blood flow from his side and scalp, it was also sapping precious heat from him every minute he stood in it.

Fighting to keep still, he tried to hear any noise above the gurgle of the water. A splash from upstream caught his attention, and he strained to hear anything more. A few seconds later, he saw a light shine on the water—and it was coming his way.

Bolan pushed forward to the edge of the plant curtain. There was a chance he might be able to improve his situation, but it would be extremely risky.

Feeling along the river's bottom, Bolan found a good-sized rock that fit in one hand. Then he moved to the edge of the hollow space under the bank. He saw lights farther up the stream, then one shone down on the water right in front of him.

Bolan froze, hardly daring to breathe. He heard a crackle of static, then a voice ask, "Sigma, you got anything?"

"Negative. Initial sweep of the west bank is coming up empty. If he went in unconscious, maybe we should look farther downriver."

During the overheard conversation, Bolan had set his rock down and slowly crawled out from under the bank, hauling himself up hand over hand. He had just pulled himself high enough to see the man's boots about a yard away, looking downstream as he spoke on his walkie-talkie.

"Continue your sweep until Beta orders otherwise."

"Understood."

In that short exchange, Bolan had gotten close enough to reach out and grab the man's feet with both hands. Taking a deep breath, he hauled back with all his strength, pulling the startled gunman into the stream before he could cry out.

The gunman fell on top of Bolan, driving him down to the streambed. Bolan couldn't see due to the disturbed water and churned up silt from the bottom. He kept his hands on the man's body, trying to either keep him submerged so he would drown or get to his throat to strangle him.

The man wasn't making it easy though, thrashing around as he tried to reach the surface. He actually managed to stand up for a moment, his head and upper chest breaking the water's surface. Coughing and spluttering, he managed to suck in a breath before Bolan reared up and tackled him, taking them both under again.

Bolan had been watching the man's hands while he was standing, and he'd drawn a knife. The Executioner grabbed his adversary's wrist. The two men thrashed around in the water, each trying to gain the advantage. Bolan knew the longer the fight drew out, the more dangerous it was for him, as sooner or later one of the others would come by to reinforce his attacker. Feeling his lungs start to burn from lack of air, he got his feet under him and pushed off the bottom, jackknifing his body forward to drive his opponent deeper underwater.

The man's struggles grew more desperate as the lack of air began to tell on him. He tried to regain his footing, but Bolan kept sweeping his feet out from under him. Finally he dropped the knife and clawed at Bolan's face with one hand as he tried to break the other man's hold. Failing at those, he flailed his arms, thrashing for the surface, his hands clawing at the water. Bolan hung on grimly, knowing how this was going to end. Eyes bulging, his face puffed, the gunman's mouth finally opened, and he swallowed a huge gulp of water. He jerked and spasmed as he drowned, his hands flapping against Bolan's face as the life drained out of him.

Bolan held the body under for another minute, letting himself up just high enough to take a breath. When he was sure the man was dead, he patted the body down for weapons. This was one of the men who'd carried only a pistol, as he couldn't find the strap for the submachine gun, and his holster was empty. Hopefully he dropped the gun on the bank, Bolan thought. As he was searching, he found the knife the man had tried to stab him with, a single-edged Gerber, stuck in his shirt. Clamping the blade in his teeth, Bolan listened for signs of anyone coming to investigate or lights approaching the area. After a slow thirty-count, he heaved the body out of the water, then pulled himself up after it.

Bolan felt all around for the pistol but didn't find it. It had to be in the water. Kneeling by the corpse, he stripped it of the camouflage jacket, web belt and dagger sheath, and started working on the boots, which were double-knotted and soaking wet. After a few seconds, he slit the laces from bottom to top and yanked them off. He tried to wedge them on his feet, but they were at least two sizes too small.

The walkie-talkie clipped to his belt suddenly crackled to life. "Sigma? Sigma, report. You're overdue." Several seconds of silence passed. "For your sake, you better be taking a leak in the woods. Sigma? Where the hell are you?"

Bolan grabbed the radio and pressed the transmit button. "Sigma's dead, and you're next. Tell your buddy Alpha I'm coming for him and the rest of your crew."

Instead of signing off or blustering, the voice answered

him. "Matt, is that you? You're more resourceful than we realized. I'm wondering exactly what it is you did before your time at the State Department—"

Bolan hit the squelch button to cut him off. "Believe me, before this is all over, you and the rest of the hopped-up crew you're running with are going to find out."

"Your bravado is impressive, but meaningless. You're alone, outnumbered and outgunned. Not to mention you no longer have any shoes. Even if you could follow us, you don't have a clue where we're going, or what we're really about. If I were you, I'd suggest you concentrate on staying alive."

A bright beam of light caught Bolan in its glare, and he dived back into the water as automatic fire stitched the area around him.

Seeing bullets slice tunnels in the water to his right, Bolan turned and swam underwater upstream until his lungs were about to explode. He looked up first, scanning the banks for lights or movement. Seeing none, he cautiously poked his nose up and took a breath. He knew he had to get out of the freezing water as soon as possible. Ears alert for any sign of movement, Bolan crept to the far bank and crawled out, heading for the nearby tree line right away. For a moment, he considered trying to double back and get to his SUV, figuring the risk would be worth it if he could reach his guns—or his smartphone, which would connect him to Stony Man Farm. However, he discarded the idea, figuring they'd probably leave a guard or search and disable the Escalade before they left. And although he was one of the best in stalking and killing silently, if they had night vision—which he didn't discount—that would give them an incredible edge. All one would have to do is get the drop on him and he'd be toast. No, it was best to flee immediately, but he definitely planned on returning to fight another day.

If he remembered the map correctly, the road was to the south—unfortunately, on the same side of the stream as the bad guys. Bolan struck out to the west, hoping to cut around them and intersect the road as it curved north.

As he walked, shivering in the soaked jacket, knife in hand, he grimaced. He knew it wasn't going to be easy flagging someone down looking like he did.

9

Arms folded, Sarah Dantlinger sat in the folding chair in Randy Jermaine's office, trying to control her temper while listening to him.

"Look, Sarah, you're a damn good ranger, one of the best I've got, but rules are rules. Pending an official investigation, I have to place you on suspension until this is cleared up."

"Dammit, Randy, that's bull and you know it. We're short staffed as it is, and there's a list of things that need to be done a yard long. The budget cuts have pretty much assured us that we're gonna be short at least one person for the season, and probably into next year. To suspend me now means the park gets screwed." She took a deep breath and smiled. "You've let other rangers work on probationary status during disciplinary investigations before."

"Yes, when the people accusing them of verbal abuse and assault didn't have a brother in law who's also a state congressman. I'm sorry, Sarah, but we can't have any appearance of impropriety right now. If they come in here, start digging and find out that I did have other park rangers working on probation during disciplinary periods, everyone could be at risk."

Dantlinger leaned back in her chair and crossed her arms. "Including you, right?"

"As the ranger in charge, sure, I'd be at risk, too."

She leaned forward, putting her elbows on her knees. "So what's to stop me from blackmailing you to put me on probation while this is cleared up? I'm already at risk—I've got nothing to lose."

Instead of looking nervous or upset, Jermaine just smiled. "That's what I like about you, Sarah. You're smart enough to see all the angles in a situation."

Dantlinger waited for him to finish, but he just remained silent, that inscrutable smile on his lips. "I get the feeling there's supposed to be an 'and' or a 'but' after that sentence."

"Right. The 'but' is that you're too upstanding to ever consider doing something like that."

Dammit, he wasn't supposed to know that! she thought. "Hell, am I that easy to read?"

Jermaine shook his head. "Of course not. I didn't have to read it in you. I see it every day in how you do your job. There isn't a crooked bone in your body. Why do you think I rely on you so much?"

"And here I thought it was my winning personality."

Her boss chuckled. "That's another story. Look, I know this guy's story is a crock of steaming wolverine shit, and I'm backing you one hundred percent. However, until we get this squared away, I still have to follow procedure." He stood and held out his hand. "I'm afraid I'm going to need your badge and your sidearm."

Dantlinger considered protesting again, but instead looked into Jermaine's eyes and realized she wasn't going to win this one. Her boss may have been more of a pencil pusher than a park ranger, but he wasn't a guy who could be pushed around. Slowly she unclipped the badge from her belt and hefted it in her hand, staring at the shield with the eagle on top, with a circle containing a buffalo under a rising sun, before holding it out to him.

Jermaine took it and pointed to the other side of her web belt. "And your gun."

Grimacing, Dantlinger truly hated to be without her pistol, she unclipped the matte-black SIG-Sauer P-220 Carry Elite Dark, ejected the magazine and set both on Jermaine's desk.

"I'll be back for all of this."

"And when that day comes—hopefully sooner rather than later—I'll be happy to give them back to you." Jermaine shook his head. "Take a piece of advice, Sarah, even though I know it doesn't play to your strong suit—be patient. You know I'm on your side and will back you all the way. I'm sure we'll be able to settle this soon. In the meantime, why don't you relax for a change. I know you've only had three days off in the last month. Your apartment's probably a wreck. Go do your laundry, watch some television—you know, stuff normal people do."

Dantlinger couldn't help smiling at his earnest plea. "I'll take that under advisement, Randy. Thanks."

"Just remember, no one wants you back here more than me. Just let this guy cool down, and let us handle it, all right?"

She nodded. "All right. It's late, I might as well head home." Dantlinger got up and walked to the door. On the way, she stuck her hands in her pocket, where her fingers encountered the 9 mm shell casing. "Hey, Randy?"

About to tackle a stack of paperwork, he glanced up at her. "Yeah?"

"This is the other reason I came in." She walked back over and set the casing on his desk. "I found this at the missing campers' site, along with some stained rocks. Might be blood."

Randy picked up the shell and sniffed it. "Inconclusive on its own. You know people can openly carry pistols into a park as of the 2010 law change."

"Yes, but they can't discharge them—that's still against the law. And what about the rocks I found?"

"That's not enough for me to put out an a BOLO, Sarah. After all, there wasn't any other signs of them there, was there? No tents or equipment, no leftover food, no vehicle, right?"

Dantlinger's shoulders sagged. "No."

"Which means the most likely scenario is probably the truth—they decided to head elsewhere, and just haven't notified their parents or friends. For all we know, that shell could be from any number of campers over the summer, and the stain, if it is blood, is more likely to be from one animal eating another out there."

She frowned. "So you're not going to follow up on this?"

"Tell you what—I'll send Mark out to the campsite if there's no sign of them come morning, and if he agrees with you, I'll mobilize our people to keep their eyes open, okay?" He waved at the door. "Now get out of here. You're off duty, remember?"

"Yeah. Good night, Randy." Dantlinger let herself out and walked across the deserted parking lot to her own car, a six-year-old dark gray Toyota 4Runner. Getting in, she sat there for a moment, staring out the windshield at the vast parkland to the south. As she looked out at the dark plains and forest in front of her, her intuition kept tickling her brain. Something wasn't right at that campsite, it kept telling her, and you know that.

Leaning over, she popped open the glove compartment. Inside, nestled in a Bianchi 7 Shadow II holster, was a black .40-caliber SIG-Sauer P-239. She removed it, checked the load and threaded the pistol and holster onto her belt. Starting the SUV, she pulled out onto the road and headed into the park.

THIRTY MINUTES LATER, Dantlinger was still ten miles away from the campsite at DeLacy Creek when her Toyota's headlights picked up a man walking by the side of the road.

And what's going on here? she wondered as she drew closer to him. The man was about six foot three, with broad shoulders and black hair. Besides the fact that he was walking down the Loop at night, he was also wearing a wet camouflage jacket that was too short for him, and he was barefoot.

No shoes in October was suspicious enough—that was usually found on stoned, shirtless hippies during the summer season—but when he saw the lights, the man darted off the road into the grassy field. That made the ranger pull up across the road, illuminating him in the 4Runner's headlights—or at least try to. Although she would have sworn she'd kept her eyes on where he had entered the knee-high grass, the guy had disappeared.

"What the hell?" Dantlinger had a million-candlepower hand spotlight on the seat next to her. Plugging it into the cigarette lighter and leaving the engine running, she got out, using the driver's door as cover, and keeping her hand near her pistol. Standing on the aluminum tube running board, she played the light over the field, looking for a crushed trail, swaying grass—anything that would indicate where he'd gone. There was no sign of the guy—it was like the empty field had literally swallowed him.

"Sir, I'm a park ranger. Are you injured or hurt? I can take you to a place that can help you." As she called out into the darkness, Dantlinger widened her search pattern until she was covering the entire 180 degrees hemisphere along the road. Nothing to the left or right either. The back of Dantlinger's neck prickled as she stared into the night.

"Prove you're a park ranger." The voice came from behind her, making her start and try to spin around. Her foot slipped, and she nearly fell off the slick side rail. Grabbing the top of the door for support, she shone the light across the top of her SUV to catch the man ducking out of sight on the other side.

"Hold it! I'm not going to hurt you!" She stepped down. "Why don't you come out where I can see you?"

"Not until you prove to me that you're a park ranger first."

Dantlinger automatically reached for her badge before remembering she had given it up less than an hour ago. "In my glove compartment over there is a pay stub from this year." She fumbled at her back pocket, pulling out the slim leather wallet she carried while on the job, flipped it open and held it up for him to see. "Here's my driver's license—those two things are the best I can do. They don't give us ID cards out here."

The man tried the door on the far side. "It's locked."

"Oh, right—sorry." Dantlinger hit the electronic release. "Try it now." Keeping her other hand near her gun, she swallowed hard, trying to calm her racing heart. The entire encounter had taken on an element of unreality. Usually she was in command of a situation the moment she appeared on the scene, but this guy had thrown her for a loop.

He'd found the pay stub, and was comparing the name on the slip issued from the U.S. government—Department of the Interior—with what was on her driver's license. While he was looking at it in the dome light, the park ranger took a good look at his face, noticing bruises and a couple streaks of dried blood on his scalp and forehead. "You're injured."

"I'm all right for now."

She noticed he was favoring his left side, as well. "Your side is bothering you, too. Were you in a fall, or some kind of accident?"

He glanced up, giving her a flash of piercing blue eyes, and his forehead narrowed a bit. "'Some kind of accident' works for the moment."

He kept scrutinizing the paper, and Dantlinger kept scrutinizing him. At first glance, there was nothing remarkable about his appearance—his short, no-nonsense haircut framed a set of features that might have been found on any number of middle managers in any company across the country. She had caught a glimpse of arctic ice-blue eyes, and found herself wondering what it would be like when they stared at her full bore. As she looked closer, she realized his face was cut and bruised, as if he had been in a fight. But even so, there was something about him....

No, it wasn't just the face, but a sense of purpose, of presence that he exuded. In any situation, whatever it is, wherever it is, he'd be the leader, she realized. Even out here, in a wet jacket and barefoot, he'd automatically assumed control of the situation. That surprised the hell out of her.

He then put the slip back and closed the glove compartment door. "Why didn't you simply show me your badge?"

"I'm—on administrative leave at the moment."

He just nodded. "Are you armed?"

"Yes."

"Good." He opened the passenger door and got inside, turning to look at her. As Dantlinger had expected, his gaze was direct and piercing, as if he held himself to a very high standard and expected everyone else around him to do the same. "My name is Matt Cooper. I work for the State Department. Like you, I don't have anything to prove it, but that's because my identification was stolen from me about thirty minutes ago by several heavily armed men who are still in the park. When they ascertained my identity, they interrogated me about my presence here and then attempted to kill me."

Dantlinger still hadn't gotten into the SUV. "Kill you? In Yellowstone?"

"Yes. You need to take me to your headquarters so I can call in and request DHS assistance. This group, whoever they are, is doing something here in the park, and I need to find out what it is." He glanced out the window at the dark road to the right. "We need to get moving. From how they were talking, I don't think we have much time."

Dantlinger slid into the driver's seat. Although she didn't have a shred of proof about his story so far, the matter-of-fact way he'd told it indicated *he* believed it. "Where did this all happen?"

"The campsite at DeLacy Creek."

That made up Dantlinger's mind. "All right, let's go. There's a clinic about twenty minutes away, as well as a lodge where I can contact my boss and you can get ahold of your people."

She put the 4Runner in reverse, executed a neat turn and floored it, taking off down the deserted road.

ARKADY NOVIKOV HAD BEEN supervising the off-loading of the nuclear warhead when the call came in. He keyed his radio. "Yes?"

"Alpha, we've located Sigma's radio. The man has flagged down another vehicle and is with a second person, a female. She appears to be a park ranger. How should we proceed?"

Novikov shook his head. While he'd expected that federal personnel might cotton to his plan, he was hoping it wouldn't happen so soon. But doubtless this Matt Cooper—who'd shown an uncanny ability to survive against incredible odds—was already telling his improbable story to the ranger. He couldn't take the chance that they might alert other authorities.

He keyed his transmit button. "Terminate the man and woman at the earliest opportunity. If you can make it look like an accident, do so. Otherwise, just eliminate them. Report in when it's finished, then return to base camp."

"Affirmative. Eta, Psi, out."

Novikov returned to the case containing the warhead. They'd set it on the ground, and the rest of the group was clustered around it. "Are the ATVs and cargo trailers ready to go?"

Zeta whistled, and a squat, four passenger six-wheeled Max IV roared out of the tree line and braked to a stop in front of them.

"Both ATVs and trailers are one hundred percent operational, Alpha," the helmeted driver said.

"All right, get the trailer attached, strap down the cargo and everyone prepare to move out." As his men and women went into action, Novikov walked over to where Beta was studying a detailed map of the area. "Are we still planning to head for our original target?"

Beta had outlined a path from the campsite to Mary Lake. "This lake lies directly on the main fault line crossing North America from Alaska to the Caribbean. If anything could cause a massive earthquake and jump start the caldera, this would be it." He jotted down the GPS coordinates on it and held the map out to Novikov. "You drop our little package in the lake and set it off, and that should start the chain reaction."

He accepted the map and nodded. "Good work, Beta. Make sure everyone has the coordinates in their GPS finders. In the unlikely event one of us is incapacitated, I want to be sure that any one of us can complete the mission."

"I'll take care of it, sir—" Beta stopped talking as a faint popping noise could be heard several miles away.

BUSINESS REPLY MAIL
FIRST-CLASS MAIL   PERMIT NO. 717   BUFFALO, NY

POSTAGE WILL BE PAID BY ADDRESSEE

THE READER SERVICE
PO BOX 1867
BUFFALO NY 14240-9952

NO POSTAGE
NECESSARY
IF MAILED
IN THE
UNITED STATES

Send For
2 FREE BOOKS
Today!

I accept your offer!

Please send me two free
novels and a mystery gift (gift
worth about $5). I understand
that these books are completely
free—even the shipping and
handling will be paid—and
I am under no obligation
to purchase anything, ever, as
explained on the back of this card.

366 ADL FMQG   166 ADL FMQG

Please Print

FIRST NAME

LAST NAME

ADDRESS

APT.#   CITY

STATE/PROV.   ZIP/POSTAL CODE

Visit us online at
www.ReaderService.com

Offer limited to one per household and not applicable to series that subscriber is currently receiving.

Your Privacy—The Reader Service is committed to protecting your privacy. Our Privacy Policy is available online at www.ReaderService.com or upon request from the Reader Service. We make a portion of our mailing list available to reputable third parties that offer products we believe may interest you. If you prefer that we not exchange your name with third parties, or if you wish to clarify or modify your communication preferences, please visit us at www.ReaderService.com/consumerchoice or write to us at Reader Service Preference Service, P.O. Box 9062, Buffalo, NY 14269. Include your complete name and address.

GE-GF-12 ▲ Detach card and mail today. No stamp needed. ▲

Novikov shared a smile with him. "That must be Eta and Psi taking care of our last loose end." The popping continued for a minute, then fell silent. "They should be reporting in any moment now." He held his radio and waited, occasionally glancing at the organized efforts around him.

Novikov felt a swelling of pride in his heart as he watched the dedicated men and women of EarthStrike go about their business, clearing the campsite and packing up their gear for the trek ahead. They were all fully aware of the ramifications of what they were about to do, and had accepted it as a necessary part of saving the planet. They had committed to giving their lives to the cause, as Iota, Epsilon and Sigma had. With these people by his side, ready to do whatever it took to complete their vital task, he could not fail.

His radio squawked, and Alpha raised it to his ear. "Eta, Psi, repeat last transmission."

The radio broke silence again, and Psi whispered into it. "Alpha, this is Psi. We have engaged the targets but encountered heavy resistance, Eta is seriously injured. Will try to terminate targets now. Will report in once mission is complete—"

The loud pop of gunfire from the speaker made Novikov pull the radio away from his ear. He heard a loud yell from Psi, followed by another burst of automatic weapons fire before the transmission ended. He exchanged a concerned glance with Beta, then turned to the rest of the group. "To me, EarthStrike commandos, right now."

The dozen men and women left in his command gathered around Novikov. He looked them all in the eye before continuing. "First, let me congratulate all of you on the completion of the first stages of our overall mission so far. Although we conceived and planned Project Rebirth with every intention of bringing it to fruition, we've already come farther than I had hoped, faster than I'd expected, and that all is due to your excellent concerted efforts."

There were smiles and murmurs of pleasure all around, and Novikov let them enjoy it for a few seconds before he continued. "However, there may still be a thorn in our collective side that needs to be removed. Although Eta and Psi are valiant warriors, fully committed to our cause, I'm afraid that this man, Matt Cooper, may still be alive, and may prove to come and try to stop us, even though we are so close to achieving our goal."

The expressions turned dark, the comments nasty and profane. Novikov held up his hand. "Although I had wanted all of you to be there at the moment we executed the final stage of our mission, I'm afraid I'm going to have to ask for three volunteers to remain at the base camp and ensure that we are not followed."

There was no hesitation—every hand in the group, including Beta's, went up. Novikov smiled at the unanimous response. "Of course—I should have expected nothing less. All of you honor me, and EarthStrike's mission, with your commitment."

He turned to Beta. "Choose two volunteers to join you and set up an ambush here. Unless Psi gives you the proper countersign when he radios in, you will kill anyone coming into this campsite."

Beta stiffened at the orders and nodded. "Affirmative, Alpha."

Novikov turned to the others. "Finish all preparations. We move out in ten minutes." As everyone scrambled to complete his or her assigned task, he flipped open his cell phone and dialed another number.

"Omicron," the voice on the other end said.

"This is Alpha. Be advised that a variable is loose in the park." Novikov passed on the description his people had given of the escaped witness. "He said he worked with the

U.S. State Department, and identification we found confirms this, but he escaped our sweep team, killing three of them in the process. He is to be considered armed and extremely dangerous. He has connected with a female park ranger and is probably going to contact the authorities."

There was a hiss of indrawn breath on the other end. "Is the operation compromised?"

"Not yet, and I've sent people to take care of the matter. However, if by some chance they manage to escape, I'm counting on you to handle them."

"It will be done."

"Excellent. Alpha out."

"Omicron out."

10

Bolan watched the woman drive with near total concentration on the road ahead. She was handsome and strong-jawed, with dark brown eyes, and her chestnut hair was pulled back in a ponytail. She seemed straightforward and no-nonsense, and hadn't even blinked when he'd told here there were armed killers loose in the park. *Which means she suspects something about them, as well,* he thought.

"Do you know anything about the people I encountered?"

She glanced at him for a moment before returning her attention to the road. "Your story—while sounding a bit extreme—kind of fits in with another incident at that campsite that happened yesterday. A group of six campers at the site went missing. When I checked it out, I found a 9 mm casing near a fairly fresh fire pit, along with some stained rocks in the circle. I thought the stains might be blood."

"You report it?"

Again that sidelong glance. "Of course, but I didn't have a survivor of an attempted murder to back me up. I expect my boss will listen a bit more closely now."

"Do you have a smartphone?"

"Yeah, but the reception is terrible out here. That's why it'll be best to use the phone at the lodge."

"May I borrow it anyway? I have to get in touch with people about this right away."

She handed her phone over with a shrug. "You can try, but you're probably not going to get through."

"Don't worry about it." Bolan activated the web browser and entered a particular web address that linked him to a satellite that would connect him with Stony Man Farm.

"Yes?" a gruff voice on the other end said. Bolan recognized the voice of Aaron "the Bear" Kurtzman, Stony Man's senior computer expert.

Bolan looked over at the park ranger. "I'm on an unsecure line," he said.

"Initiating security protocols." Bolan heard a slight tone on the line, and knew that the conversation was currently being encrypted at both ends. "I thought you were on vacation?" the wheelchair-bound computer genius asked.

"Yeah, so did I." Bolan quickly filled in Kurtzman on what had happened to him earlier that evening. "I need you to run a search on militia groups in the western U.S. that may have the funding and resources to field a platoon-sized group of men, armed with automatic weapons and the latest comm equipment, that kind of thing."

"I'm on it." He heard clicking in the background as Kurtzman entered his search parameters into the Stony Man computers. "What about you? Need back up? Calvin and Gary just got back from their latest field work. I'll see if they're available." He referred to Calvin James and Gary Manning, members of Phoenix Force.

"It'd be a good idea to get them on the first flight out here, although that's going to take a while, even flying into Jackson Hole. We're running out of time. I may have to go in alone."

"Well, let me see what I can do for them on the Stony

Man Express. I take it you're sticking around there?" Kurtzman asked.

"Oh yeah. You know how mysterious people trying to kill me always piques my curiosity."

Kurtzman's deep voice rumbled as he chuckled. "Yeah. How you fixed for gear?"

"Poorly, although I'm with a park ranger who's going to alert the locals and hopefully fix me up." That comment earned him another sidelong glance.

"That I can't help you with on such short notice, but I'm sure you'll be able to fend for yourself. I'll contact Hal."

"Hey, a day without Hal worrying about where I am and what I'm doing is like a day without sunshine." A gleam in the side mirror caught Bolan's eye. "I have to sign off, Bear. I'll call in when I get the chance, hopefully when we're back in civilization."

"Keep your powder dry, Striker, and try to keep us informed. I'll get Calvin and Gary wheels-up ASAP."

"Thanks." Bolan cut the connection and checked the mirror again. "How far away is that clinic?"

"At this speed, about fifteen minutes. You concerned about the vehicle following us?"

Bolan's estimation of the woman's abilities rose another notch. "Correct."

"Well, the road's too winding to lose them, so if they're gonna fuck with us…" She drew a compact pistol from a holster at her side and handed it to him. "Since that didn't sound like any branch of the State Department I've ever heard of, I assume you can handle this?"

Bolan checked the load and the action. "Forty caliber. Very nice."

"Nine mil doesn't have the stopping power I want."

"Out here, I suppose not, if you have to take down something larger than a person." Bolan appraised the gun with an eye that had seen thousands of them in his lifetime. "You take good care of your weapon."

"That and a hundred rounds a week on the range will buy you a cup of coffee."

Bolan's eyebrows raised again. "Indeed."

They drove on in silence, each keeping an eye on the fast-moving lights behind them. "I'm sure they're coming after us. You'll probably want to buckle up."

Without taking her eyes off the road, Dantlinger drew her seat belt over and clipped in. "There's a spare mag in the glove compartment. Sorry there isn't more, but I never expected to have to fend off armed gunmen."

"First time for everything." The high beam lights from behind them lit up the entire cab of the 4Runner, and the pursuing SUV—a squat, heavy Chevy Suburban outfitted with a heavy steel ram bar on the front—came right up to their bumper, then roared forward, crashing into the 4Runner's back end.

Bolan and Dantlinger both lurched forward in their seats. "I guess that means they aren't gonna invite us to dinner," the ranger said with a strained smile. She accelerated, but the powerful Suburban easily kept up with them, slamming into the lighter 4Runner's rear bumper again. "I'm open to any ideas you may have to dissuade them."

Bolan hit the electric window lever on his side, letting the chilly night air inside. "I prefer a direct application of lead to the problem. Slow down a bit—lure them closer."

He turned in his seat and waited while Dantlinger complied. As expected, the Suburban confidently approached their decelerating target. "Okay, here they come...hold her steady."

Pistol held in a two-handed Weaver grip, Bolan popped out the passenger-side window and drew a bead on the driver's side of the Suburban's windshield, part of his mind noting their pursuers were driving without any lights on.

As soon as the sights lined up, he squeezed the trigger as fast as he could, putting five shots through the glass—and hopefully the people inside—in less than three seconds.

The Suburban swerved with the third shot and slewed onto the gravel shoulder, tires squealing and brake lights flashing as the driver fought for control. He retreated about fifty yards away before straightening and driving back onto the road.

"Did you hit anyone?" Dantlinger asked.

"Don't know. Just keep driving. How far now?"

"It's still about eight miles away."

"I don't think they're going to let us get that far." As if in answer to Bolan's comment, a series of loud, fast pops burst behind them, and they heard loud thunks as bullets hit the back of the SUV, shattering the rear window.

"Swerve! Swerve!" Bolan shouted as he ducked into his seat. Hunching, Dantlinger wrenched the steering wheel to the left. The 4Runner's left tires shrieked as they hit the gravel shoulder, making the Toyota spin out and lurch to the left. Easing off the gas, Dantlinger steered into the skid until she could regain control without flipping the vehicle.

"Jesus, that wasn't a pistol!" Breathing hard, Dantlinger checked her rearview mirror to find their pursuers.

"I told you they were carrying automatic weapons. Nice job on the evasive driving."

"Thanks, but we're not gonna last too long against that." She continued to drive in a flat S-curve down the dark road.

The first burst was followed by a several more. Dantlinger evaded as best as she could, but one of them ended in a loud bang and the 4Runner's left rear corner settled as the thumping of a flat tire filled the shaking SUV.

Dantlinger looked back and frowned. "Damnit, he got my tire! I'd just replaced them a month ago!"

"If they catch up with us, that's the last thing you'll have to worry about." Grabbing the spotlight, Bolan climbed into the middle seat. "At the next straight stretch of road, kill your lights."

"What?"

"Just trust me!"

"Okay…" They rounded another curve, then the 4Runner straightened. Bolan got into the rear cargo compartment of the SUV, extending the spotlight's cord as far as it would go. He hunkered down behind the rear door, painfully aware of how little protection it afforded against the automatic weapons they were facing.

"When I say so, I want you to turn around as fast as you can and drive straight back at them."

"Into submachine-gun fire with a flat tire. Are you clinically insane, or does this just happen when people start shooting at you?"

"Some would say a bit of both." Bolan hit the floor as another burst of bullets caromed off the roof. "They're running without lights, which means they're using night vision. I'm holding a million-candlepower spotlight. You do the math."

"Now you're talking. Just tell me when."

"Not yet." Bolan peeked up over the door frame to see the Suburban coming closer, the passenger leaning out his window and readying his submachine gun. When they drew within twenty yards, Bolan raised the spotlight and flipped it on, aiming the dazzling beam directly at the Suburban's windshield. "Now!"

He heard an agonized scream, and the gunner threw his arms up and slid back inside the SUV. Instead of braking as he'd expected, the driver accelerated, coming straight at Dantlinger's 4Runner. She'd just slammed on the brakes and cranked the wheel hard over, putting the Toyota into a controlled slide that almost turned them completely around. Hitting the gas, she roared back down the road—directly at the Suburban.

Bolan had popped up in the back and was firing at the driver's side again as fast as he could pull the trigger. As they raced by the SUV, he saw a splash of red spray onto the windshield and knew he'd tagged the driver. Ducking, he reloaded the SIG. "Turn around and go back!"

Dantlinger stood on the brakes, which were now making a terrible grinding noise, and cranked the wheel around again. The Toyota vibrated as it revved toward the Suburban, which had drifted to a stop by the side of the road.

"Stop here." Dantlinger pulled off the road about ten yards behind the truck. Bolan was out of the vehicle before it stopped rolling. He approached the SUV on the rear driver's side, coming up to the rear bumper, then stopping and listening for any sounds of movement in the cab. Hearing nothing, he edged around to the side and slowly began moving up to the driver's door, staying low to minimize being seen in the side mirror. At the rear passenger door he paused, then quietly reached out and tried the door handle. It was locked.

A burst of bullets erupted from inside the SUV, destroying the window and punching through the metal near his hand. Bolan hit the dirt and crawled forward to the driver's door. Looking up, he took a half-step away, then placed the pistol next to the closed door, about where a man's torso would sit in the driver's seat, and pulled the trigger three times.

He heard an anguished shout from inside, and Bolan moved back just as another burst of bullets shattered the driver's window, perforated the door and sparked off the road where he'd been crouched. Hearing the engine try to turn over, he gambled that the passenger was trying to start the SUV, and popped up to stick the pistol into the back of a hunched over head.

He was right. The passenger of the Suburban was half-sitting on the body of the driver, who was covered in blood, and trying to start the SUV. When he felt the barrel of the SIG-Sauer press into his neck, he froze and raised both hands.

"Very good. Now listen to me and do exactly as I say. I'm going to open the driver's door. When I do, you are going to get out of the vehicle and lie on the ground, hands on your head. Any offensive action or move I don't like on your part will result in your brains splattering on the windshield. Nod if you understand."

The man nodded.

Bolan popped the door, which resisted at first, but he managed to force it open. "Come on, then."

The gunman crawled out over the driver and onto the ground. His weapon, an HK MP-5, was swiftly liberated by Bolan, who checked the magazine's load, then cycled the action.

Dantlinger ran up, and Bolan gave her pistol back. "Cover him." While she did, he checked the driver, who was slumped in the bucket seat, very dead. A terrible hole in his neck had caused him to bleed out, covering his black fatigues and web gear in blood. Of the three shots Bolan had put through the door, two had hit him, as well, drilling deep into his side. On the rear passenger seat Bolan found another loaded HK MP-5 with two extra magazines. He slung that one over his shoulder and shoved the magazines in his back pockets. Next he grabbed the keys, dragged the driver's body out and to the back of the SUV. Opening the back doors, he heaved the corpse inside, and was about to slam the doors when he noticed the man's combat boots.

A minute later, his feet clad in broken-in boots that fit like they were made for him, Bolan walked back to Dantlinger and their prisoner. Rummaging around inside the passenger compartment, he came up with a roll of duct tape and walked over the other man, a towhead who looked to be about thirty years old. "Hands behind your back." The man complied, and Bolan secured his hands, then slapped a strip across his mouth.

Dantlinger stared at Bolan's activities with wide eyes. "We should keep going and get to the Old Faithful clinic—"

"Where's the nearest campground from here?" he asked.

"Scaup Lake is a couple miles back, but I need to report this—"

"Maybe, but right now my first priority is to find out what the hell is going on out here." Grabbing the young man by his arm, Bolan dragged him to his feet, eliciting a groan of pain. "Look, you've been a big help so far, and I'm not going to ask you to go any further," Bolan said to Dantlinger. "In fact, you probably should head back to that clinic and report in, since I think we might need a hell of a lot more people out here before this is all over."

"What are you planning to do?"

Bolan herded his captive into the passenger seat and bound his legs with duct tape. "Like I said, I need to find out what these people are up to. To do that, I'm going to that campsite you mentioned and interrogate him."

"Shouldn't we arrest him and take him to jail?"

"If this were an isolated incident, I'd be all for that, but he's part of a larger plot, and I need to know what that is and what their schedule is. Like I said, you should probably head back and summon more help."

"And what are you going to do with the information?"

"That depends. If there's time to get a law-enforcement group assembled, then we'd go after the group and try to capture them. But if whatever plan they're executing is in its final stages, then I'm going in pursuit and taking them out."

Dantlinger frowned. "What the hell? You're a government agent. I thought vigilante justice died out in the last century."

"These guys are well financed, armed and trained. They aren't running around Yellowstone for training exercises, they're here for a reason, and I'm going to find out what that is."

Yanking open the passenger door, Dantlinger climbed in. "If they're as dangerous as we both think they are, then we're gonna need help. We're only a few miles away from the Old Faithful clinic, and you need to have those wounds looked at. All I'm asking for is thirty minutes. Let me see if I can raise my boss and get some reinforcements down here before we go charging into the forest on some potential wild-goose chase."

Bolan tried to pierce right through her with his eyes, but Dantlinger held firm, not dropping her gaze for an instant. Despite the gravity of the situation, he was impressed by her reaction. "I've seen far too many things like this go down—these guys are for real, I promise you that."

"If they are, that's all the more reason to enlist as much help as we can get."

Bolan narrowed his eyes at her. "I could leave you here and take him and their SUV and go do this myself."

She nodded. "You could, but in your condition, I have some doubts as to how successful you'll be going up alone against such a well-armed and equipped force. Look, I've trusted you so far based solely on your word—and because two people just tried to kill us. Please, grant me the same courtesy so we can get some help."

"All right, we'll head to the clinic, but I'm keeping my prisoner until I've interrogated him."

As soon as they were rolling again, Dantlinger got on her phone, trying to reach ranger headquarters. The system on the other end rang and rang.

"Randy might have gone home for the evening already, so if he doesn't answer, you might get your wish." The answering service clicked on, and Dantlinger was about to leave a message when she heard the click of the receiver being picked up.

"Yellowstone National Park Rangers, Mammoth Hot Springs Headquarters, how may I help you?"

"Randy?" Dantlinger breathed a sigh of relief. "It's Sarah."

"Hi, Sarah, you just caught me. I was about to head home—"

"Randy, listen to me. That bullet casing I found at the campsite, it's connected to something a whole lot bigger."

"What are you talking about?"

"Just listen." Dantlinger filled him in about finding Agent Cooper along the road and then gave his story. She follow that up with the two gunmen who had tried to run them off the road and kill them.

"Wait a minute—you say you're with this Cooper right

now, and have one of the alleged shooters in the back of the stolen SUV?"

"When you see what they did to my 4Runner, you'll know it's not alleged shooting, Randy."

"Okay, okay. Where are you now?"

"We're about a mile away from the Old Faithful clinic. I'm taking Cooper there for medical attention."

"Shouldn't you both come up to the clinic at Mammoth?"

"No, this was the best compromise. Cooper believes these two groups are part of a larger operation that's going on in the park, and wants to call for reinforcements and go after the rest of them as soon as possible."

"Okay, get him to the Old Faithful clinic and keep him there. I'm in Norris right now. Your call got forwarded to me, and I'm coming down right away. I'll meet you there. Until we ascertain exactly what we're dealing with, don't speak with *anyone* else about this. It's off-season, but we still don't want to cause a panic among the locals. It's thirty miles away. I'll be there in twenty minutes."

"All right, we'll be waiting for you inside. Thanks, Randy."

"Hey, no problem, Sarah. Just sit tight, and I'll be there in a jiff."

Bolan looked over. "What's going on?"

"My boss is coming to Old Faithful clinic to coordinate with us. By the time you get patched up, he should be there, and we can decide how best to proceed."

"All right. We're here."

The businesses at Old Faithful consisted of the clinic, a small general store, a gas station and three lodges. Directed to the clinic by Dantlinger, Bolan pulled around to the side of the building and parked. She got out and joined him at the back of the SUV.

"Just a minute." Bolan opened the doors and quickly

created a duct-tape rope that he used to tie their captive's hands to his feet. "Don't want him trying to break a window or attract anyone's attention." He made sure the man's mouth was securely covered, then closed and locked the doors again. "Let's go."

They walked in the front doors of the clinic, and were greeted by a bored-looking young nurse who quickly perked up once she got a look at Bolan's wounds. "Uh, we're actually more of a walk-in clinic. Perhaps he'd be better served at Mammoth—"

Bolan cut her off. "Nurse, this is a matter of national security. If you can direct me to a doctor on duty, please do so at once, as it is imperative that I receive treatment and get released as soon as possible. If you cannot do this, then please supply me with antiseptic, gauze, bandages and tape, and I'll clean and dress my wounds myself."

The raven-haired woman drew up with a sniff. "Sir, that would not be appropriate procedure. As these seem to be gunshot wounds, they will have to be reported to the proper authorities—"

Dantlinger broke in. "Thank you, Nurse, that's being taken care of right now. If you could show us to a treatment room while we wait?"

She led them to a waiting room with the traditional accoutrements of a doctor's office. "Wait here. The doctor will be in to see you in a few minutes."

The moment she was gone, Dantlinger began rummaging through the cabinets.

Bolan watched her for a moment. "What are you doing?"

"Here, a few minutes can be as long as a half hour. Get your shirt off if you can without aggravating that side injury, and I'll have a look at it."

Bolan was able to remove his shirt without too much pain, and after she'd laid out the necessary tools,

Dantlinger bent over to inspect the wound. "You've seen your share of action."

"Goes with the territory."

"I'll bet." Dantlinger cleaned Bolan's side wound, which turned out to be a nasty, blood-filled furrow under his ribs, and dressed it. Then she turned to the head wound, taking no chances, testing his vision and checking for a headache. This injury turned out to be a graze, carving a flap of skin off his skull and tearing a lot of vessels. "Lucky you—a half inch over, and it would have fractured your skull. As it is you're lucky you don't have a concussion," the park ranger said as she applied another antibiotic-infused bandage, taping it securely in place. When she was finished, she tossed him a knit cap. "Found this in the SUV. To cover the white bandage, and keep you from losing too much heat up top."

"Thanks." Bolan stood and stretched experimentally, testing the placement of the bandage on his side. "You do good work."

"I tried to keep it comfortable, since I expect we'll be on the move for the next several hours."

"Yeah." Bolan's head swiveled as he heard fast footsteps approaching, and a moment later a harried-looking man in a National Park Rangers jacket and shirt entered the room.

"Randy, thank God you're here. Matt Cooper, Randy Jermaine."

Bolan offered his hand, which was shaken perfunctorily by the newcomer, then dropped. "Looks like they've taken care of you pretty well here."

"Well, your ranger has," Bolan replied as he pulled his shirt back on. "It's her work."

"Of course. That training really does pay off. Why don't you both come with me to the ranger station, which is right next door? We can talk privately there."

Bolan followed Jermaine and Dantlinger to the ranger

station, which was a small room attached to the clinic. Randy closed the door between the two places and waved them both to a pair of green folding chairs. "All right, Sarah's apprised me of the situation, but if you don't mind, Agent Cooper, I'd like to hear your version of the events that happened earlier this evening."

Bolan gave a terse rundown of what had happened, starting with the men at the campsite and ending with them arriving at the Old Faithful clinic. When he was finished, he added, "Now that my wounds have been taken care of, we need to assemble a law enforcement team to go there and round up the rest of the group."

"Steps are being taken to address that right now, Cooper. I just have a couple of questions first. You said that you fled the campsite without any firearms, is that correct?"

"Yes, but there are several illegal fully automatic weapons in the SUV."

"Right, thank you for that information." Jermaine turned to Dantlinger, and she was surprised to see a trickle of sweat drip down the side of his face. "Now, Sarah, I know you didn't use your service weapon during the chase on the Loop. What gun did you give Agent Cooper?"

"A personal weapon that I carry in my 4Runner."

"And where is that weapon now?"

"I have it." Bolan withdrew the SIG-Sauer from his coat pocket and set it on the desk.

Jermaine picked up the compact pistol and put it in a drawer. "Thank you. Do either of you have any other weapons on your person?"

Dantlinger and Bolan both shook their heads.

"Good." Jermaine stood up, a familiar-looking pistol in his hand.

Dantlinger frowned when she saw it. "That's my service weapon. Randy, what's going on?"

"I want both of you to stand slowly, keeping your hands in plain sight at all times."

Dantlinger's eyes nearly bugged out of their sockets. "Randy, what the hell are you doing?"

"Oh, Sarah, why didn't you head home like I'd asked you to? You just had to go poke your nose into where it didn't belong, didn't you?"

Still sitting, Bolan narrowed his eyes. "Of course—that's why they were able to get into the park so easily. I should have realized earlier. Sarah, your boss is working with these guys."

"Is that true, Randy?"

Her boss's smiled tightly. "I'm afraid so. Things cannot continue as they are going—the center cannot hold, things fall apart. If someone doesn't take action soon, it will be too late, not just for our generation, but for the planet."

Dantlinger frowned. "What the hell are you talking about?"

Jermaine seemed to get hold of himself, shaking his head. "Never mind. All right, here's what's gonna happen. You two are gonna walk out this exit door and we're going to your SUV, where you're going to free that prisoner. Then we're all going to take a drive out to the DeLacy campground, and Alpha will decide what to do with both of you." He waved the pistol toward the door. "Cooper, you first. And just remember, I'll have my pistol pointed at the back of Sarah's head. Any false moves, and she'll be the first to die."

"Don't worry about me." Bolan slowly rose and walked to the exit.

"You next, Sarah." Jermaine was sure to keep at least four feet from Dantlinger, too far away for her to try to grab the pistol.

Dantlinger slowly rose. "Why, Randy? All of us work

here because we love the park and nature. What do you hope to accomplish?"

"This may seem hard to believe, but that's exactly what I'm preserving by stopping you two. Cooper, when you step outside, walk two steps forward and stop. Keep your hands at your sides, visible to me at all times."

"All right." Bolan stepped out, watching their captor out of the corner of his eye.

"Now you, Sarah." She complied, and Jermaine closed the door behind him. "Let's go to your vehicle, nice and easy. No one make any sudden moves. I'd hate to have to shoot either of you through the kidney."

Dantlinger glared back at him. "I'd hate for that to happen, too."

"All right, from now on, no speaking unless you're directed to. At the SUV, Cooper will open the back doors and step away. Once the other man is free, we'll take that ride."

DANTLINGER'S PULSE hammered in her head as they approached the Suburban. She knew once the captured man was free, the chances of them subduing both him and Jermaine were much slimmer. If anything was going to be done, it would have to happen in the next few seconds.

She stole a glance at Cooper, who was walking a few steps ahead of her, too far away to be any immediate help. She figured he'd assist her once she made a move. A t least, she hoped he would. She just had to plan it right.

They'd reached the SUV. "Slowly and carefully now, Cooper, take out the keys and open the door." Jermaine stood to the side, the pistol still aimed at Dantlinger, but able to cover Bolan in a second if necessary.

Dantlinger slowly took a deep breath then let it out, centering herself as she rehearsed the actions in her mind. Step....pivot...hold...throw.

The federal agent hit the Unlock All button on the SUV's remote, and the door locks opened with a clunk and a loud beep.

The moment she heard that beep, she moved.

Stepping backward, Dantlinger simultaneously pivoted to bring herself inside Jermaine's range. She almost came face-to-face with him and saw him staring at her through startled eyes. He started to correct his aim, but it was too late.

Grabbing his gun hand at the wrist, Dantlinger made sure it wasn't pointed at the agent while moving into position by turning so her back was to Jermaine. She crouched and pulled forward, yanking him off balance. As he hit her shoulder, she dropped it while pulling his arm down, sending him flying over her to crash to the pavement. Still retaining control of his arm, she twisted his hand back until she could remove the pistol from his trembling fingers, still keeping him on the ground with the wristlock.

The entire movement had taken less than a second.

Bolan had popped open the back doors and was at her side, duct tape in hand. "Nice move." He slapped a strip over Jermaine's mouth, then quickly bound his hands and feet. "You okay?"

"Yeah. What are we doing with him?"

"If we had more time, I'd interrogate both of them and see if their stories matched. But since he's delayed us even further, we'll just secure him in his office and come back for him later. It'll be good to have a witness to all of this later who can tell the Feds the whole story." Slinging Jermaine over his shoulder, Bolan carried him back into the ranger's station and lashed him securely to a folding chair, then placed him in the closet. "That ought to hold him for a while."

Dantlinger was still a bit stunned at what she had just done. "I can't believe he was a part of this."

"You saw it just like I did." Bolan walked behind the desk and opened the drawer. "I believe this is yours." He held out Dantlinger's SIG-Sauer pistol.

"Thanks." She tucked it back into her holster. "Should we still try to contact outside help. Other rangers? The police?"

Bolan shook his head. "Too dangerous. We wouldn't know who else might have thrown in with these guys."

"Well, then, I guess we do it your way from now on. Let's go."

Bolan drove along the Loop until they came to the Scaup Lake campsite, which was also deserted.

"Most people stay in the lodges this time of year," Dantlinger said as they pulled in.

"Good, less witnesses—and questions—that way." Bolan killed the engine, grabbed the HK subgun, got out and drew his dagger. Opening the rear passenger door, he cut the bonds on their prisoner's feet, then hauled him out of the backseat. Pushing the guy ahead, Bolan marched him to the nearest picnic table and sat him at a corner. Kicking his feet near the leg, he swiftly wrapped the man's legs to the table, immobilizing him.

"What are you planning on doing?" Dantlinger said, trailing behind him.

"I'm going to interrogate him."

"How exactly?"

"It's simple." Bolan ripped the tape off the man's mouth. "I ask him a question—" he pulled back the cocking lever on the HK "—and he answers. If I like what I hear, he keeps all of his body parts. If not, well, a human being can live an awful long time with two-thirds of their blood and several joints with bullets in them."

"Whoa, whoa, whoa. I can't sit by and let you in good

conscience shoot this guy to get information on some kind of suspected terrorist operation you only think might be happening."

"Then perhaps you should take a walk for a few minutes." Bolan turned and led Dantlinger a few yards away, standing so the guy couldn't see his face. "I don't really want to torture this guy, but he's got information we need, so I'm going to try to break him psychologically with the threat of violence."

"But if he calls your bluff, you're not gonna go through with it?"

Bolan hesitated, then shook his head. "There's a line for everything, and I don't descend to the level of terrorists."

"All right, then. Are you thinking of going 'good cop, bad cop' on him?"

Bolan cocked his head at her. "Sure, if you're up to playing the good cop."

Dantlinger nodded. "I think I can handle that."

"Excellent, that might help get what we need sooner. Do you still have your smartphone?"

"Yeah, why?"

"Let me use it again, if you don't mind."

"Sure." Dantlinger handed it over. "Why?"

"There's someone I want to hear our little Q and A." Bolan dialed Stony Man Farm again, getting Kurtzman on the other end.

"That was quick, Striker. Don't tell me you wrapped things up already?"

"Not so much, Bear. Listen, I've got one of their men isolated, and I'm about to interrogate him. I'd like you to listen in on the conversation."

"Hit the speakerphone and have at it."

Bolan did so, and tested the reception. He nodded to Dantlinger. "Okay, we're a go." He walked back with her and set the smartphone on the picnic table. "This interrogation is being recorded. Interrogators are Matt Cooper, State Department, and Sarah Dantlinger, U.S. Park Service. Subject is one—" Bolan patted the man down but came up with empty pockets. "Identify yourself."

He'd expected to get only sullen silence out of the guy, but was surprised. "Michael. J. Arneson, EarthStrike member since 2004."

Bolan heard the faint tap of keys from the phone and knew Kurtzman was cross-referencing the organization's name with the federal database of known terrorist organizations. He continued. "All right, Mr. Arneson, our conversation can be pleasant, or it can be difficult. It all depends on you."

"As you are an official representative of the U.S. government, and I assume that I am already or am about to be placed under arrest, I request access to a lawyer, and that you read me my Miranda rights."

Bolan's lips peeled back in what could charitably be called a smile. "That's all well and good. Mr. Arneson, however, as you may have seen, we haven't taken you to a proper detainment facility. Nor are you receiving your one phone call, and, well, there just aren't that many lawyers out here in the woods. As I said, this can go easy, or this can go hard." He flicked the safety off the HK MP-3 and pressed the muzzle to the sitting man's forehead. "But when you tried to kill Ranger Dantlinger and myself back there, you made it hard for yourself. Now, I'm going to start asking questions, and you'd better give me some answers I like, otherwise the bullets are going to start coming your way."

Dantlinger intervened, lifting the submachine gun's barrel away from the man's head. "Jesus, Matt, you said you were going to ask him questions, not just put the gun to his head and threaten to blow his brains out. For God's sake, let's try to conduct this civilly, all right?"

Bolan twisted his face into a scowl and stepped back. "Hey, I'm just giving him the same chance he and his buddies gave us on the road back there. But if you're so concerned about 'violating his civil rights,' then go ahead and coddle him all you want!"

"Just let me ask him a few questions first." Dantlinger sat next to Arneson. "Michael—do you prefer that, or would you rather be called Mike?"

The man smiled and shook his head. "It doesn't matter. You two think I don't know what you're up to?"

Dantlinger frowned. "What do you mean?"

"This good cop, bad cop routine. It's right out of central casting. He's the mean hard-ass, you're the nice lady cop who I'm supposed to build a rapport with so you can get the information you need. Your psychological mind games are all so pointless. None of it will matter in the end."

"Why not, Michael?" Dantlinger asked.

The former gunman stared at Bolan for several seconds, then nodded at him. "He's a prime example of 'why not.' Standard government agent, swallowing their lies about dancing to their tune 'for the good of national security' and maybe even 'protecting the innocent' or freedom, or some such crap like that. He's gone through his life not questioning what he does or why he does it, but performs on command, just like a trained dog."

Bolan grunted. "Nothing I haven't heard before from a thousand guys just like you."

"Oh, Agent Cooper, I doubt you've heard everything I have to say."

Arneson held his gaze for a few more seconds before turning his head to regard Dantlinger. "You, on the other hand, I might believe has more capability for independent thought, since you're out here, trying to protect the remaining wilderness. But, unfortunately, you and your fellow park rangers are also part of the big machine, the

United States government, which smiles benevolently at its citizens while all the while hiding the corruption, the backroom deals, the government and national corporations who are always let off after raping the landscape, polluting the environment, poisoning its own people. And when they are 'caught,' usually because their actions grew far too egregious to sweep under the carpet any longer, they're exposed to the public for the charlatans and destroyers they are. And what's their punishment? They pay a fine of a few million or tens of millions of dollars—it's always a drop in the bucket to them—and are allowed to go about their business like nothing ever happened."

"I've heard enough to know what you are," Bolan strode back over to put his face right next to Arneson's. "Hardcore ecoterrorists, willing to destroy the planet to save it. You guys preach your 'one Earth, we're all brothers' manifesto, but you're just in it for the thrill of destruction while you hide behind your so-called manifesto, claiming to be doing this to save the planet."

"Damn it, Matt, would you lay off? I apologize for Agent Cooper's behavior, Michael."

Arneson didn't reply to the characterization, which surprised Bolan. In fact, he was strangely calm. "You're right about the 'ecoterrorist' aspect of it, Agent Cooper, but you couldn't be more wrong about the rest."

Bolan pulled back from him and crossed his arms. "Well, why don't you enlighten us, then?"

"Gladly." Arneson leaned back on the picnic table, smiling as if recollecting a fond memory. "Crazy as this will sound, I had my first moment of clarity about humanity and the environment back in 1999, while at the movie theater, of all places."

"Oh, how so?"

"There I was, watching *The Matrix*, the first one. And there was that scene where the agent program had captured the wise mentor guy, Morpheus. Anyway, before Morpheus gets captured, the agent is talking to him, describing the human race as similar to a virus, in that it multiplies until it consumes the resources of an area, then moves to another area and does the same thing."

Arneson shook his head. "It blew my mind. I mean, here was the *bad guy* saying this, yet at that moment I totally sympathized with him. I understood exactly what he was talking about! What was even crazier was that I *agreed* with him!"

"Is there a point to all this?" Bolan asked.

Arneson fixed him with a smile that was chilling. "Oh yes, Agent Cooper, there is. You see, once a person accepts this fact as the truth, then one must accept the additional truth that humanity will keep spreading and spreading, eventually inhabiting every part of the Earth until it has consumed all of this planet's natural resources."

Dantlinger shook her head. "Wait a minute, that's not the case today. Reproduction rates in many populated areas—Europe, Japan, even parts of the U.S.—are declining."

Arneson shrugged. "Isolated pockets of population stability or decline are no match for the ever growing Third World. Anyway, no matter what anyone says, this planet is not limitless—our resources are finite. At some point, humans will use up everything here, and where will that leave us?"

Bolan thought the question was rhetorical, but Dantlinger answered. "Assuming you're correct, the remaining people will be subject to starvation and susceptible to famine, plague, war for whatever resources are left."

"Exactly. Humanity will drive itself to extinction and take the planet with it, until this world is nothing but a polluted, toxic, barren wasteland devoid of all life except perhaps insects."

"Sounds like you've been reading too much science fiction yourself, buddy." Bolan advanced on him. "All I know is that I'm getting tired of you talking without having anything to show for it."

Arneson smiled and nodded. "True, Agent Cooper. You've been most patient with me, and for that I will reward you. This idea consumed me—it became all I thought about, talked to other people about it, searched the web for more information on. As I did, my eyes were opened to the terrible things that are being done to this planet in the name of advancing a country's status, or despoiling an area or region for the sake of profit."

Bolan got right in Arneson's face again and said, "So far I'm not hearing anything that I can use, Mr. Arneson."

"I'm getting there. During my research, I delved deeper and deeper into the environmental movement, looking for like-minded individuals who shared my concern for what humans were doing to this planet. I studied quite a few, joined others, but none understood the underlying issues at hand, nor were as committed to taking whatever action was necessary to stop it. Then I found EarthStrike, a group of individuals who shared my belief and the idea that something could still be done about it, with the proper equipment and planning."

"Finally—" Bolan was shushed by Dantlinger, who nodded.

"Go on, Michael. What can be done about the planet's situation?"

He smiled sadly at her. "Traditional methods are like a child trying to contain the ocean with a sand dam. Americans, and anyone who gets a taste of the First World life are hard-pressed to give it up. Draconian measures like limiting the number of children a family has in order to inhibit population growth lead to terrible acts of brutality against women and innocent children. Off-world colonization is, unfortunately, a pipe dream, as there is not the overwhelming need nor the funds available to truly make it work. And even if we did, who's to say we wouldn't end up doing the same thing on another planet? As for trying to work through the government or law—" he turned a baleful eye on Bolan "—even if substantive legislation could be passed through the maze of special interests, corporate lobbyists and pork-barrel bureaucracy that infests Washington, D.C., it would be watered-down or rendered toothless or ignored by those it was meant to regulate."

"And I suppose, Mr. Arneson, that you and your group have come up with a plan to change everything?"

Arneson nodded. "Yes, Agent Cooper, we have. The more I researched, the more I realized that humanity could not, would not be turned from its present course of action. Therefore, there is only one prudent solution to be implemented."

"And that is?" Dantlinger asked.

"If you have blight on a fruit tree, you treat it with pesticide to kill the invaders without destroying the host. If you have an infestation of termites in a house, you treat the place with insecticide to kill them while retaining the structure. When it comes to the planet Earth, however, it's a little harder, but there is still a way."

Exchanging a troubled glance with Dantlinger, Bolan voiced their conclusion first. "Are you saying you and the rest of the EarthStrike crazies out here are planning to exterminate the entire human race?"

Arneson looked at him with a calm, serene expression. "That, Agent Cooper, is exactly what I'm saying."

13

Bolan's question and Arneson's answer hung in the air between the three people for a few seconds. Dantlinger broke the silence first.

"You're serious, aren't you, Michael?"

He nodded. "Yes, as is every one of us in EarthStrike. Each member was exhaustively probed and tested to confirm their commitment to the cause—that of saving our planet by whatever means necessary."

Bolan frowned. "Don't tell me you guys arrived at the idea to kill all humans first?"

"Believe me, we exhaustively researched all possible alternative theories and plans, from starting new colonies in deserted areas of the world—or even off-planet—to bringing the world's scientists together to figure out a way out of this slow trek toward extinction, to conjecturing some way to capture the world's attention and drive the point home that we are slowly killing our planet." Arneson's shoulders slumped. "But there was no way to realistically get the message across to a large enough segment of the population. Sure, some people would listen, but the majority of people live for themselves, and maybe their families, in a day-to-day existence. More concerned with ensuring that they and their immediate family are cared for, they don't take the time to look at the larger picture. Over the course of developing our plan, we realized that one of the great things about it was that trying to reach the masses, and then coming up with a viable way to implement the needed changes wasn't necessary. Our solution would be a baseline event that would affect everyone, regardless of their location, ability, or social status."

"What the hell does that have to do with what you're planning?" Bolan snarled.

"The difference, Agent Cooper, is once you cease to factor the reaction of the target populace, when you cease to think of them as individuals and look at humanity as one singular, diseased biological being, putting us out of our misery is the only sane thing to do, right?"

Bolan couldn't believe he was hearing this. "Even if I agreed with you for a second, which I don't, how do you expect to do this?"

"For a brainwashed government drone, Agent Cooper, you ask very good questions." Arneson took a deep breath. "First, a bit of history. Are both of you aware of the Toba catastrophe theory?"

Bolan shrugged, but Dantlinger answered. "Yes, that's the theory that humankind went through a population bottleneck approximately seventy-three thousand years ago, when the supervolcano erupted at Lake Toba in Indonesia. The resulting ash cloud, volcanic winter, and climate change reduced the world's population to anywhere from three thousand to ten thousand people, who then began reproducing and repopulating the planet."

"Exactly. Our plan is simple—recreate the Toba event and let the resulting chips fall where they may."

Dantlinger stared at him, her eyes wide. "You mean you people think you can make the Yellowstone caldera erupt?"

Arneson nodded. "Yes. As we speak, a nuclear warhead is traveling toward our ground zero, and once it's reached its destination, it will be detonated, ideally making the supervolcano we're all standing on right now, which, according to geologists, is several thousand years overdue for another eruption. And then we can watch the ash fall like rain. However, being this close to the ground zero, most likely we'll be killed within the first three to five minutes of detonation."

Dantlinger slowly shook her head, as if she could somehow refute what she had just heard. "My God...the ash cloud would cover at least two-thirds of the United States and Canada, and prevailing winds would carry the fallout around the world. You would condemn billions of people to starvation and death. You people are nothing more than psychotic monsters."

Arneson shook his head sadly. "That is often the reaction of the short-sighted. Perhaps I didn't make myself clear, Ranger—we are talking about nothing less than the survival of the planet itself. A person, or one billion people are nothing more than a virus on the surface of a very sick world, which is growing sicker all the time due to our ceaseless efforts to suck it dry. Me, you, him, everyone in American or around the world means less to us than one square foot of unspoiled grassland, a healthy tree growing on the African savannah, even a fly buzzing around doing what it does best."

"But wait a minute—you'll also destroy tens of thousands of miles of various ecologies, not to mention wipe out thousands of animal species." Bolan frowned. "How in the hell do you reconcile that with your extinctionist agenda?"

"Acceptable losses when you look at what's at stake. Just because an animal exists does not mean it is guaranteed to survive to the end of its natural evolutionary process. Humans are no different. In the end, it's simple enough. Those who are left will create a world where Darwin's elegant theory will play out as it always has—the fittest will survive in this new world, and those who are not capable of adapting shall perish."

Arneson looked from Dantlinger to Bolan. "Don't you understand? Earth will finally have a chance to heal itself, and as humanity itself is incredibly adaptable, we have no doubt that there will be survivors—albeit a fraction of the population that existed before. It will be up to them to create a new world out from the ashes of the old one. I only hope they will do a better job than we did with our stewardship of this planet."

Bolan stared at the man so hard that if his eyes were lasers, he'd have easily bored through Arneson's head. "Who do you people think you are? Who made you the stewards, to use your own phrase, of the planet? Who gave you the right to decide that humankind doesn't deserve to live any longer? That you people, and you alone, know what's best for this planet?"

Their prisoner shook his head. "That is exactly the response I expected from you, Agent Cooper. Who gives anyone any power in this world? I certainly don't want the U.S. government doing a lot of the things it does, but it goes ahead and does them anyway, often to the detriment of the world at large. No, we came to the decision a while ago that if we were ever going to effect change for this world, we'd have to do it ourselves. And don't think this is for posterity, or because we're trying to draw attention to the world's plight with what you think is this crackpot scheme. It doesn't matter if future generations hail us as saviors or damn us as destroyers. In the end, we will have *done* something, we will have made a difference—and that's what will matter."

Stalking over to the man, Bolan grabbed him by the front of his shirt and hauled him close to his face, though the man's movement was limited by his taped legs. "You and your insane friends aren't going to ever have the chance to make that new world, because I'm going to stop them. When I'm through, you'll be lucky to get a brief mention on the eleven-o'clock news."

Arneson chuckled. "No, I'm afraid you aren't. You're too late—they've already started their trip to ground zero, the location of which I don't know. No one knew except for our leader, and he hadn't told us before we were dispatched to kill you. You can torture me all you want, but it won't help. All you'll be doing is letting the rest of my group get closer to their destination, and from there it's only a few minutes until the bomb is detonated. You're already too late."

"Hold that thought." Bolan grabbed the smartphone and stalked a few yards away. "Bear, you get that?"

"Every word, Striker."

"What's the probability that this guy's spouting the truth?"

"It's hard to say. Out of everything he said, he's right about one thing—the thirty-four-mile diameter caldera is technically due for another eruption. Geologists believe it goes off about every six hundred thousand years, and the last one occurred about 640,000 years ago. The fallout from such a pyroclastic explosion is what's hard to determine. I'm sending you estimated fallout maps of what the average eruption would do to the North America."

Bolan logged on to a cloud-based e-mail address and opened the link Kurtzman had forwarded. The picture wasn't pretty. For hundreds of miles in every direction, from Minnesota in the east, to most of Texas in the south, to California in the west, the fallout cloud would envelop all of the middle third of the United States.

Bolan shook his head. "Jesus."

"Yeah. What I can tell you is that it would cripple the United States, destroy the breadbasket of North America, and kill hundreds of thousands of people within weeks of the initial eruption. Then the ash would carry in all directions due to the prevailing Jet Stream, affecting Canada, Europe and beyond. The aftereffects are harder to gauge, but they include a long volcanic winter, possibly six years or more, drastic climate change around the world, and mostly likely widespread crop failure, leading to food shortages, riots, and the inherent conflict derived from those flash points. If they did seed the fault line running through the park with a warhead of sufficient magnitude, the worst-case scenario is that the detonation could spark a chain of eruptions that could last for years. If that happened, it could very well mean the wholesale destruction of the human race," Kurtzman said.

"So at the least they reduce America to a Third World country, probably setting off a lot of conflict around the world and at the worst case, they hit the reset button on the entire planet."

"Those are the two outcomes, yes."

"Based on what you've heard, do you think they can really pull this off?"

"That's the big unknown, Striker. No one's sure what will happen if you set off a nuke on a fault line or in a volcano. The bottom line, of course, is that even a moderate eruption would be devastating to the immediate area and its surroundings, probably hundreds of times more destructive than the St. Helens incident. It's far too risky. They have to be stopped."

"I'm right with you on that one. What can you tell me about this group EarthStrike."

"Yeah. Details on these guys are really sketchy. No web page, and they're barely mentioned in the ecoterrorist webrings I've been having Akira infiltrate. Near as we can tell, they consist of about fifteen to twenty members who, if the net rumors are to be believed, are behind some of the more deadly ecoterrorist acts of the past several years, like the tree trapping in the Pacific Northwest." Bolan was aware of that one. Logging companies there had been menaced by unknown assailants who cut through trees until they were almost going to fall over, then leave them to be downed by the vibrations of machinery and cutting of other trees. It caused three deaths, seven injuries and hundreds of thousands of dollars in collateral damage.

Kurtzman continued. "Supposedly they're also behind the flooding of a natural gas company's headquarters with four tankers of tailings from one of their mines. I don't know how in the hell they managed that. The only person I've been able to connect it with is a Russian, and that info came straight from Moscow, believe it or not."

"Who is he?"

"A guy named Arkady Novikov, from the Ural Mountains. Get this, he's ex-Spetsnaz, served the motherland from 1991 to 2004, then dropped off their radar when his mother died. They're looking for him, too, so I have the feeling that if you were to take him out, the Russians wouldn't be crying too hard about it."

"That explains why these guys are so well trained. That also complicates how we can take them out."

"There are a couple of ways, actually. We can't activate a wide-scale assault on these people, as it could cause them to detonate the device prematurely, which could still have devastating effects on the continent. So there's no helicoptering in reinforcements or anything like that. Also, there's probably not a lot of time to round up additional search members before they place and detonate the warhead."

"What about an air strike option from…where's the nearest Air Force base, Malmstead, in Montana?"

"That's correct, however, even if we flag this a priority one situation, I'm concerned that briefing the proper people and getting clearance won't happen in time to prevent the detonation. I'm alerting NORAD and the Air Force brass right now, but we both know it's up to you to stop them."

"That's the plan, except this guy claims he doesn't know where they're headed to plant the bomb."

"Since you first checked in, I've been scoping out the area and have picked up nine GPS signals heading north of the DeLacy Creek campsite at a steady pace. Real-time intel indicates it's a group surrounding two six-wheeled vehicles, one towing a boat, the other hauling something shaped very much like a warhead. I'm willing to bet the rest of my life that they're your guys."

"Great work, Bear. Can you extrapolate where they're headed?"

"Computer simulations give a seventy-four-point-eight percent chance that they're headed for Mary Lake. It's in the middle of the Loop, in the upper west quadrant of the caldera. However, it's located on the major fault line that runs diagonally from Alaska to the Caribbean Sea. It makes sense—if they sink it there, they place the bomb closer to the fault line, and the water pressure would also create a sort of improvised cover, directing the majority of the explosive force down into the earth. Don't get me wrong—hundreds of thousands of gallons will be vaporized, and even more will be spewed into the atmosphere, but if they're trying to maximize the yield of the blast, they've thought this out pretty well."

"Too well to let them get away with it. What's their current location?"

"They're approximately three miles north of the campsite and less than eight miles from the lake itself. You'd better get a move on if you're going to intercept them."

"We're heading out now. Roust Hal and get him to kick this up the chain, and we'll keep you informed as to our progress. Striker out."

"Good luck."

Bolan broke the connection, then walked back to Dantlinger and their captive. "All right, my contacts have given me the most likely destination they are heading to, given the area. We are moving out to intercept right now."

Arneson's mouth dropped open in shock. "You're bluffing."

"Nope. Your buddies are heading toward a place called Mary Lake, about ten miles north of here."

"What— That's not possible. How?"

"Never underestimate the resources of the U.S. government. We're heading out in five," Bolan said.

"Before we go, you need to have those wounds dressed. If they reopen while we're out there, I don't want to be responsible for dragging you around and chasing these guys, too."

Bolan couldn't argue with that logic. "All right. There's probably equipment in the Suburban. One thing I'll say for you guys is that you came prepared."

"What about me?" Arneson asked.

"Well, once we stop your buddies, you'll be charged with breaking a whole lot of laws regarding domestic terrorism. However, if you want to start helping us, that may mitigate the length of your final sentence." Bolan doubted that but thought he might get some short-term cooperation from this guy anyway, which was why he'd dangled the possibility.

Arneson regarded Bolan for a long moment, then hung his head. "You know the main party's moved out, but there's probably a few left behind at the launch point, to make sure you don't get any farther. If you let me radio in, I can clear the way for you so they won't try to ambush you."

"All right, we can try that, but I'll be holding the radio,

and if you try anything funny, the gun will be in my other hand, you got it?"

"Yeah—yeah, I understand. Before I call, do me a favor—fire two shots in the air, then another one a few seconds later."

"No way. That's probably the signal to your buddies that you've been captured."

Arneson shook his head. "Look, if you want this to work, there has to be a good reason why I've been out of contact for so long. If I tell them I had to chase one of you into the woods and finally got you, there'd better be some gunshots to go with it."

"You get one." Bolan readied the radio, then switched the MP-5 A-3's fire selector to single-shot, pointed it toward the night sky and fired a single round, the report rolling out over the hills and into the mountains.

Arneson began panting, and he motioned with his head for Bolan to bring the radio over. "This is...Psi reporting in...can anyone at base hear me...hello, is anyone there?"

"Psi, this is Beta. What is your status?"

"I...eliminated one target on the road...the woman fled into the forest...I had to chase her down...I just put a bullet...into her head."

Bolan glanced over to see how Dantlinger was taking the matter-of-fact report of her death. The park ranger stood with her arms folded, staring at their prisoner, her face impassive.

"What is your status?" Beta asked.

"I'm all right...and back at the SUV...I'm returning to the launch point, over."

"Did you recover the bodies?"

"The woman is a half-klick in the woods...I left her... am bringing the man's body back...as well as Eta's."

"Affirmative, we'll see you upon arrival. Beta out."

"Roger that, Psi out." Arneson blew out a deep breath. "There. Well, you got what you wanted, didn't you?"

"Not even close. Only when your buddies are caught or dead and their nuclear payload are secure will I have gotten what I wanted."

"So, when am I being taken to jail?"

Bolan knelt to cut his bonds, then prodded him up with the barrel of his gun. "Not yet, buddy. We might still need you, so you're coming with us for now. Back in the SUV."

With Dantlinger covering from a distance, Bolan tossed him into the back of the Suburban, tied his feet again and slapped a patch of duct tape over his mouth, then slammed the door shut.

"Nice acting back there, by the way."

Bolan shook his head. "A lot of it wasn't acting."

"Ah. So, you think they're setting a trap for us?"

Bolan headed for the driver's door. "I guarantee it."

"How do you know? He didn't give any kind of code that I heard."

"That's the problem. A good commander establishes codes that work whether or not you say them. For home-grown soldiers, these guys are some of the best I've ever seen. The fact that he didn't say anything out of the ordinary means he probably tipped them off that he's been captured."

"Holy shit! Why didn't you say so? So, we're gonna avoid them, right? I mean, if we start from here and head north, we can cut these crackpots before they reach the lake."

"Afraid not, and here's why. First, I'm not going to leave these psychos for another ranger, or God help them, innocent bystanders to find. It would be a slaughter. Second, if we did leave them there, and they got wind we were after the main group, they could come up and trap us from behind, driving us into the lead force." Bolan checked the load on his HK subgun. "No, the best way to handle this is to go in and take them out while we still can."

"But driving head-on into an ambush? We'll be cut to pieces!"

"I'm not planning on dying just yet. Look, you can head back for reinforcements at any time. Stick around or head out, it's up to you."

Dantlinger shook her head. "These guys have to be stopped. I'm in till the end."

"Okay, we need to make up light packs and be sure to have them ready to toss out of the SUV. Let's go."

AT THE DE LACY CAMPSITE, Beta switched his radio to the alternate channel and hit the transmit button. "Alpha, this is Beta, come in."

"This is Alpha, over."

"Regret to inform you that Psi has been captured by the enemy. They will be coming to the launch site in a few minutes. We will engage and terminate as previously instructed."

"Affirmative, Beta. If you can save Psi, so do, but anyone with him must be eliminated. Alpha out."

"Understood. Beta out."

14

Five minutes later, Bolan and Dantlinger stood outside the Suburban, which was presently pointing down the road toward the DeLacy site, its lights and engine off.

"I can't believe they didn't post a lookout on the road," Dantlinger whispered as she stowed the small packs she'd put together in the ditch.

"Remember, they think we have no idea what's waiting for us down there. They're probably all cozy and hidden, expecting us to drive in and offer ourselves like cows to the slaughter. Little do they know what's really coming at them. You comfortable with the night vision gear?"

Dantlinger nodded. "I've used it before, thanks. Hell, this is better than the gear we have in the helicopter, that's for sure."

"Good. We'd better get ready." Bolan opened the driver's door and ran a flashlight over their preparations. "How you doing, Mr. Arneson? Comfortable in there?"

Arneson glared at him and would have replied if his mouth hadn't been covered by duct tape. He was securely fastened in the driver's seat, his body wrapped in tape to keep him sitting, and his feet anchored to the seat by a cocoon of duct tape. Bolan had rigged up a crude steering mechanism using bungee cords to keep the SUV rolling straight. "You see what we got planned for you, don't you? I'll bet you'd like to give that clear code right now, wouldn't you? Sorry about your passenger, but he's the best we could do on such short notice."

Bolan had hauled out the body of the man called Eta and propped him up in the passenger seat, belting him in place to keep him upright.

Dantlinger watched their prisoner make muffled noises behind his gag. "I'm not sure I feel so great about this."

"If we don't have at least two people in here, it won't look right. So it's either him or us, and I don't have any plans to get shot any more today than I already have been. Besides, the only thing you have to remember is if they'd had their way, we'd both be dead on the road back there."

Bolan made sure Arneson and the body were secure, then turned back to Sarah. "Okay, let's review the plan one more time. We send our duct-taped driver and his dead buddy straight into the campsite, where either one of two things happens. First, they shoot the hell out of the SUV, in which case we know their firing positions, and can sweep in from the road and take them out. Second, if someone keeps a cool head and goes to investigate the driver, we can take him out at the vehicle, then wait for return fire and try to outflank the shooters. We'll have to move fast, since they'll have night vision as well, so surprise will count for a lot. You ready?"

Dantlinger took a deep breath, then glanced at Arneson in the driver's seat. She pressed her lips together and nodded. "Ready."

"All right, get on the gearshift." Bolan opened the driver's door and turned the ignition key, letting the engine roar to life. Turning on the headlights, he readied a short branch he'd cut on the gas pedal. "You set?"

Dantlinger had gone around to the passenger side and climbed in over the body, her hand on the shift knob. She gulped, trying not to look at the corpse only a few inches away. "Yeah."

"Here we go." Bolan jammed the stick onto the gas pedal, making the engine race. He hit the lights, then closed the door. "Do it!"

Dantlinger dropped the vehicle into Drive and rolled out as the SUV shot forward into the campsite. Bolan flipped down his night vision to track the vehicle's progress. Almost immediately it began taking fire with rows of bullet holes stitched across the hood and shattering the windshield. Bolan saw Arneson jerk and twitch as several bullets found him as well.

He glanced back at Dantlinger, who was doubled over in the road, throwing up. "You all right?"

Spitting to clear her mouth, she nodded. "Sorry—first time near a fresh body."

"You're doing fine. If you want to wait, I can probably—"

Straightening, the park ranger readied her HK subgun. "Let's move out."

Bolan led the way into the scrub brush and scattered trees off the road, creeping up on the first shooter, whose bursts of automatic weapons fire glowed like a blowtorch to Bolan's fifth-generation night-vision goggles. He looked to the side as he bobbed and weaved from tree to tree, getting to within fifteen yards before the firing began to slow. Before it could stop, Bolan snugged the butt of the MP-5 A-3 into his shoulder, flipped the fire selector to 3-round burst and pressed the trigger once.

The trio of bullets sped out at more than thirteen hundred feet per second, hitting their target less than a tenth of a second after leaving the barrel. They shattered his right arm and kept going, tumbling through his upper torso to shatter his collarbone and ribs and tear large furrows in his lungs. The gunner collapsed, already drowning in his own blood.

Bolan waved Dantlinger off to the right. The second shooter was at the rear of the campsite, with the third one on the far left side. Bolan ran to the first shooter's spasming body, kicking his gun away and taking up the position, hoping to fool the others into thinking their man was still alive. After snatching the radio from the body's belt, he let off a burst into the riddled Suburban, which had rolled to a stop over the fire pit, minus the front windshield and driver's window, its grille, hood and front fenders covered with bullet holes. Steam leaked from its punctured radiator as it settled on its two blown front tires.

"Dammit, Gamma, cease-fire, they're dead!" someone yelled over his radio. Bolan aimed at the shooter to his left and triggered two bursts. The man dropped his gun and fell to the ground. The Executioner tried to draw a bead on the last one, but he'd changed positions and was no longer visible, hidden behind the hulk of the destroyed SUV.

Bolan's captured radio crackled. "What the fuck? Who's still shooting? Gamma? Xi? Report, dammit!" He dodged and weaved through the trees, breaking out of the forest and sprinting to the SUV for cover. A burst of fire thunked into the rear of the Suburban's body. Bolan dropped to the ground, searching for any sign of the shooter, but saw nothing. He fired a couple of 3-round bursts into the forest and was rewarded by return fire hitting the SUV. Come on, Dantlinger! he thought, firing again.

For a moment, silence fell over the campsite. Then two weapons fired almost simultaneously. Bolan rolled out to the back of the SUV, scanning the tree line for any sign of movement. A body staggered out from behind a tree and then collapsed. Bolan got up and headed for it, his submachine aimed at the still form's head. "Dantlinger?"

"On your left." He glanced over to make sure she was

all right, and found her approaching with her weapon leading. "I think I got him."

As they converged on the fallen gunman, Bolan heard a loud wheezing, and the man rolled over on his back. Dantlinger had indeed hit him. His chest was a mass of blood-soaked clothes.

"Don't move!" Bolan stepped up and kicked the man's gun away.

The shooter, who Bolan recognized as Brian, the man who'd tried to have him killed at his campsite earlier that evening, smiled, his teeth dark and bloody in the moonlight. "Couldn't…even if…I wanted to…" He convulsed, and a gout of blood dribbled down his chin. "You won't… stop them…too far ahead…"

"We've taken out eight of your force so far, and I'm not stopping until all of you are dead, and that warhead is recovered." Bolan relieved the fallen man of his radio. "Wouldn't want you warning your leader that I'm coming for him."

Brian's chest hitched as he fought for breath. "The world…will be reborn…we will be…the catalyst for a new age…" His last breath left him, and his sightless eyes remained fixed on Bolan, who reached down and checked for a pulse.

"He's gone. Gather all the weapons and spare ammunition you can find in two minutes." Kneeling next to the corpse, Bolan patted down his pockets until he came up with a ring of keys, then looked back at the undamaged 4x4 Chevy Silverado crew cab pickup truck with the empty trailer on one side of the clearing. "Hope you don't mind a little damage to the local environment, but we're about to go off-roading."

"Compared to the alternative, I think we can waive the fine I'd normally write you." Dantlinger ran from body to body, stripping them of submachine guns and extra magazines. While she was doing that, Bolan removed the trailer and checked the pickup's fuel level. She joined him and dumped the armload of weapons and ammo in the backseat. "That's all of it."

"All right, let's go." Bolan slid into the driver's seat, inserted the key and turned it, sparking the big Hemi engine to life.

"Too bad they don't have any horses." Dantlinger buckled up in the passenger seat, then grabbed a bottle of water and twisted off the cap, draining half the bottle before passing it to Bolan. "We're only gonna be able to take this about six miles in, then the terrain is too rough to drive."

"Every foot we can get closer to them driving is one less we have to walk." Draining the water bottle, Bolan tossed it in back, adjusted his night-vision gear, then put the Chevy into gear and zoomed into the forest, slaloming between the trunks of tall ponderosa pines.

SECURELY BUCKED into the passenger seat, watching out the windshield as her companion deftly navigated the pickup through the forest without using any lights at all, Dantlinger took a deep breath and tried to sort out her emotions about the past several minutes.

If push came to shove, you could always say you were coerced by this guy, she thought. Well, at least until you shot that man. She still wasn't sure quite what to make of that. There was no doubt in her mind that they'd intended to kill her and Cooper both if he hadn't come up with the best way to draw them out.

For that matter, Randy would have shot us, too. That thought was even more sobering, that a man whom she'd worked beside for three years could harbor such a terrible secret, and be working to destroy everything she and the other park rangers held dear. She didn't know how she would be able to look him in the eye without feeling completely betrayed.

Dantlinger stole a glance at Cooper, who was intent on carving out a path into the wilderness, not sure what to make of him, either. Once the ambush trap had happened, it had all gone down seemingly in seconds. The Suburban getting shot up in the clearing…Cooper killing the man on the right and taking his place…Dantlinger circling around and getting ready to take out the man in back, only to see him shudder and drop after taking two bursts from the agent's gun…her finishing the sweep and coming on the third shooter, who was distracted by Cooper shooting at him from the disabled SUV. It had almost been too easy to creep up, put his chest in the circle sight on the HK subgun and squeeze the trigger.

Banishing the image of the man crumpling to the ground, Dantlinger let air whistle between her teeth as she looked at her de facto partner again. The matter-of-fact way he'd handled everything from the moment they'd met had led her to believe that if he was with the State Department, she was about to win the lottery. Special Forces definitely, maybe even a SEAL or Delta Force.

"So, Cooper, what are you really doing out here?" she asked.

Without taking his eyes from the outside, he shook his head. "I told you earlier, I was supposed to be on a camping trip."

"Really? This was all just coincidence that you happened to be here when these eco-nuts put their plan into action?"

"I know, hard to believe, isn't it? This is how I know the universe has a really perverse sense of humor."

"Who do you really work for?" Dantlinger asked. "The Army? Special Forces? Delta Force?"

He turned to look at her, the night-vision goggles giving

his face an eerie, bug-eyed look. "Why do you want to know?"

"More curiosity than anything. There's no way you're with the State Department—their lawyers and PR department could never spin the way you handle situations."

That last comment earned her a wry smile. "You're correct about that, but I'm not with any official branch of the U.S. government."

Dantlinger frowned. "You're not private security, are you?"

"No. I've crossed paths with them, both with and against, more than once as well. The best way to put it is that I'm a 'floater,' available to handle certain jobs that the government needs handled, but can't be involved in."

"I see. More of that 'behind-the-scenes deals' that Arneson was complaining about?"

"He did have a valid point regarding that. Sometimes our government does things that I don't agree with, but at the same time I have to trust that they're striving for a greater good overall. No matter how flawed our system is, it's still the best one we have, and I'll always do my best to uphold the principles it stands for. To think that wholesale dismantling of it will make things better is wishful thinking. All that leads to is anarchy."

"So you meant everything you said during our conversation with him?"

"I'm not sure you could hold me to every single word I said back there, however, I certainly believe that no one person, or even a group, has the right to arbitrarily decide whether a large portion of the world—or even the entire human population—should live or die. That's not a decision that any person or organization has the right to make, and I'll do whatever necessary to ensure that the nightmare scenario he described will never come to pass."

"Amen to that." Taking a firmer grip on her submachine

gun, Dantlinger stared out into the dark forest as they raced deeper into it. As she looked around, she realized what a blast of the kind Arneson had been talking about would do to this virgin forest, and she made up her mind to do anything—even if it meant sacrificing her own life—to stop it from happening.

A FEW MILES FURTHER ON, Novikov's radio beeped insistently, and he signaled his driver to brake to a stop as he lifted it to his mouth. "This is Alpha."

"Alpha, this is Lambda."

Novikov pressed his lips together. He'd been hoping to hear from Beta. That his rear guard, stationed a half-mile back, was reporting in at this time probably meant he didn't have good news. "Go ahead, Lambda."

"I've spotted a pickup truck coming through the forest, approximately three miles away. It looks like it's following our path. Attempts to raise the team at the launch site have been unsuccessful. What are your orders?"

"Continue to follow along our trail until you meet with the team I'm sending back to you. They'll have further instructions." Novikov signaled his driver to stop the six-wheeler's engine and waved for everyone to gather around him.

"Our enemies are proving to be more resourceful than I had anticipated. They have escaped the ambush at our launch site, and even now are heading toward us. They must not be allowed to draw any closer to us. Here's what I want."

He pointed at three of his team. "Chi, Epsilon and Zeta, you three will fall back and rendezvous with our rear guard. Use your rifles to take out the enemy's vehicle, then move in and kill them both. I want confirmation of their dead bodies before you call in. Are there any questions?"

The three shook their heads. Novikov nodded. "Then go, and kill these interlopers."

He watched them head out, a faint concern creasing his brow before he turned back to his driver. "How far are we from the detonation site?"

"Approximately three point six miles, sir."

Novikov nodded again. "All right. We'll double-time the next mile, then we'll set up another surprise for these two—in the very unlikely event that they survive the next thirty minutes. Let's move out."

As they got underway again, Novikov couldn't help casting one last glance at the forest behind them. He'd spent years training his force in the most ruthless ways of executing a goal, yet this nameless nemesis and his female companion were cutting a swath through them like they were raw recruits. For the first time in his life, Novikov experienced a new emotion—fear. Fear that they might not complete their mission.

Nonsense—we have come much too far to let a single man, or even two people stop us now, he thought. *We will—we must—prevail!*

15

Ten minutes later, Lambda met with the three reinforcements, and they sketched out their plan to stop the intruders. The sniper of the group, Chi, listened with only half an ear—all he cared about was that he was about to get to shoot something.

They were in an area where the flat plains were starting to give way to successively steeper hills that then gave way to bluffs before coming to the actual mountains in the area. Once he'd gotten his assignment, Chi quickly searched out the best vantage point to get a bead on the approaching vehicle. He found it in a bluff that rose almost ten yards high and faced due south, giving him a superior firing position over a 130-degree arc, and out to two miles away.

Making sure his weapon was secure over his shoulder, Chi began climbing, scaling the rock face like a monkey. As he did, he remembered the kill that afternoon, taking the man's head off at five hundred yards, the body dropping to the ground before the crack of the suppressed rifle had echoed off the hills. His groin tightened with pleasure at the vision.

As fanatically committed to EarthStrike's plan as the rest of the members, Chi had come to them straight after an eight-year hitch in the Marines followed by a dishonorable discharge for striking a superior officer. He'd come home to find his house foreclosed, his wife taking their kids and disappearing, and him too damaged by his missions in the Gulf War to hold down a civilian job. Alpha had literally found him on the streets of San Diego and reshaped him into their lead sniper. It was a position Chi relished, and he was amazingly good at his job, able to block out all distractions, until there was nothing else in the world but what he could see through his scope—a world of targets.

Atop the bluff, he found the ideal firing spot and laid out his weapon, a .50-caliber Bushmaster BA50 bolt-action carbine, with a third generation Night Optics USA 10x D-830-3A Day/Night Weapon Sight attached. Extending the bipod, he loaded his 10-round box magazine, inserted it into the receiver and chambered a round. Converting the scope to night use, he lay behind his weapon, checked out the forest floor beneath him once more, spotting his three team members, then radioed in.

"Chi in position."

The plan was simple—once they had visual confirmation on the vehicle, Chi would take it out with a round to the engine block, and, if possible, take out one of the occupants as well. If not, he would provide harassing fire while the other three moved in and eliminated the enemy.

Settling in to wait, Chi became motionless, his eye fixed to the night-vision sight, awaiting that all important order to fire.

THE PICKUP GROWLED as it clawed its way up a small hill. Inside, Bolan and Dantlinger swayed back and forth as the tires scratched and spun on the uneven terrain. Both of them were getting eyestrain from their constant scanning of the forest, searching for that lone bit of information that would alert them to an ambush.

Dantlinger finished her latest sweep and pushed up her goggles to rub her aching eyes. "You really think they'd leave more men behind to waylay us? For all we know they've already reached the lake and dumped the bomb."

"If they have, then there isn't much we can do about it, but until I see that with my own eyes, we're moving forward. As for another ambush, since we've foiled every attempt by them to stop us, and this Arkady Novikov character is way too much of a professional to leave a loose end like us floating around, I'd say we are definitely heading into another one." Bolan glanced at her through his own night vision. "Besides, it's what I would do."

"Do you do this a lot—charge headlong into potential enemy fire?"

"Actually, I prefer not to when I can help it. In a situation like this, there are far too many variables arrayed against us. Sometimes, however, when time is a factor, there simply isn't a choice."

"How do you stand—" was all Dantlinger got out before the front of the pickup seemed to bend down, then the hood flew off the frame of the vehicle as the engine literally exploded in front of them, spraying pieces and parts as the engine ground itself to useless junk. Shrapnel starred the windshield, destroyed both front tires and tore off the side mirror on Bolan's door. A gout of flame erupted from the split block, quickly spreading toward the passenger compartment. The truck skittered to a halt after a few yards, the steering wheel spinning uselessly in Bolan's hands.

Huddled in her seat, Dantlinger removed her hands from her ears. "What the fuck was that?"

Bolan shoved an MP-5 subgun at her. "High-velocity round, probably .50 caliber. Get behind the seat now!" Without waiting for her reply, he grabbed her by the shoulder and yanked her back with him into the crew compartment. As the report from the rifle died away, they heard the thunk of small caliber rounds impacting the back of the pickup. "They're all around us!"

"What now!"

Bolan grabbed a small pack and thrust it at her. "We have to evac right now!"

"Are you crazy? They'll shoot us down outside—" Dantlinger flinched as another round blew through the engine, sending burning oil ten feet in the air. The instrument panel erupted in jagged shards of plastic, making Bolan and Sarah duck as fragments pinged against the glass over their heads.

"They'll shoot us or burn us to death in here, too!" Bolan shouted back as the rear windshield disintegrated under a burst of bullets, showering them with glass pebbles. Pulling a road flare from his own pack, Bolan rose to a crouch. "I'll toss this out the back, hopefully screwing up their night vision, then follow it out. Give me a five-count to draw their fire, then go! Hit the ground and crawl to the tree line. Ready?"

Dantlinger nodded.

Bolan ignited the flare, careful to look away from it and tossed it out the back. "Start counting!" He poked his HK out the shattered window and fired three bursts, then dived into the pickup bed.

"SHIT SHIT SHIT! One...two...three...four..." Dantlinger's count was interrupted by the boom of the sniper rifle again. The truck rocked with the report, and suddenly the back was filled with chunks of foam. She stared at the fist-sized hole the bullet had torn in the driver's seat before she continued punching through the back wall of the passenger compartment.

"Fuck this!" Reaching up, she clawed at the back door handle and shoved it open just as another round tore through it, shattering the window and tearing it off one hinge. She bolted, scrambling out the opening and hitting the ground with a thud. Remembering her companion's advice, she crawled as fast as she could to the nearest copse while trying to keep her MP-5 up and ready. Although the medium submachine gun had never felt particularly heavy, at this moment it weighed her hand down like a ton of bricks.

Reaching the small cluster of trees, she huddled behind one of them, scanning her surroundings for attackers. Automatic weapon fire roared on the other side of the ruined pickup, which was completely ablaze, hindering her night vision. The sniper had stopped shooting, but Dantlinger knew he was still out there, waiting. The nearest cover was a pair of trees about five yards to her left, and after taking one more look around, the park ranger hugged her gun to her chest and rolled that way.

She had just reached the trunks when she saw a combat boot step into her vision. Dantlinger looked up to see a face covered in night-vision goggles looming above her. She tried to line up her weapon to shoot, but it was grabbed and torn out of her hands before she could squeeze the trigger, the masked attacker throwing it into the darkness. The person followed it with a boot stomp aimed at her face, but Dantlinger blocked it with a forearm, redirecting the attack and making her opponent stagger off balance. She followed up with a knuckle punch to the crotch, but instead of contacting the sensitive equipment of a man, her fingers encountered a smooth groin of a woman!

Despite hitting her solidly, her masked opponent recovered fast. She grabbed Dantlinger's extended arm, trying to twist it into an arm bar around her leg. Dantlinger lashed out with her booted foot, connecting with the woman's head and making her stagger backward. The park ranger rolled to her feet and turned to face her opponent, who was already coming back at her. Dantlinger fell into her judo stance, but the woman, who was a couple inches shorter, stopped a few feet away and fell into a stance mirroring hers.

"The only killing I got to do was a hiker bitch yesterday," she said. "But a park ranger—that's something else entirely. I'm gonna enjoy this."

Dantlinger didn't bother replying, just watched her hands, trying to gauge when her attacker was going to strike. The woman feinted high, then tried to grab her jacket collar to bring her close. Dantlinger brought her arms up and around in a circle, sweeping the woman's hands loose, then trapping them between her arms and her side. The moment she had them pinned, she brought her head forward, slamming her forehead into the other woman's face mask. But her opponent dodged, and Dantlinger hit her shoulder instead.

The woman wrenched her hands free, then grabbed Dantlinger's shoulders and pulled her down to the ground face-first. She stepped around her to place her feet astride Dantlinger's back. Knowing she was doomed if the woman pinned her, Dantlinger swept her left arm out and up with all the force she could muster. She hit the back of the woman's leg hard, forcing it off the ground. Caught off balance, the woman fell heavily on top of Dantlinger, her head near the park ranger's butt.

Dantlinger quickly pushed off the ground and rotated her hips, trying to flip the woman to the ground and catch her head in a lock between her thighs. But her attacker rolled with the attempted takedown and turned it into a somersault, rolling out of reach and rising to her feet. "You're better than I expected."

Again, Dantlinger didn't waste words on her opponent but moved forward, hands ready to strike or grab, feet placed precisely with every step for maximum balance. Her blood sang in her ears, and her body almost thrummed with the desire to beat the crap out of this bloodthirsty fighter. In the back of her mind, she realized that she might have to kill her, but she shoved that thought away, concentrating on the here and now. Knowing the person in front of her had participated in killing the missing hikers only made her blood boil even more, but she channeled her anger into controlled energy, all of it directed at her opponent.

Dantlinger had observed enough about her enemy to realize she was an offensive fighter, and figured putting her on the defensive might throw her off her game. She advanced in a controlled rush, feinting with her right hand while trying to secure a hold on her collar to throw the woman. She fell for the feint, blocking with her left hand. But instead of resisting further, the woman's right hand snaked down to her belt and came back up with a knife, slashing at Dantlinger's chest.

Forced to abandon her attempted move, the park ranger released the woman's clothes and swept the knife hand to the side while moving with the arm to control it and keep it in motion. Repositioning herself, Dantlinger brought her knee up and the knife arm down, slamming the forearm against her leg and knocking the blade loose.

Unfortunately, she'd left herself open to a counterattack, and suddenly felt a heavy blow crash down on the back of her head. It was followed by another powerful shot that drove her to her knees. Shaking her head, Dantlinger opened her eyes to see the sole of the woman's combat boot zooming at her face. Before she could block or dodge, it slammed into her cheek, sending her sprawling on her back.

Stunned for a moment, Dantlinger felt a heavy, crushing weight descend on her neck and opened her eyes to see the woman settling down on her upper chest. "You were pretty good, ranger bitch, but I'm better. Time to end this."

She increased the pressure on Dantlinger's throat and her lungs began screaming for air. The park ranger tried to reach for the woman's face but couldn't get her hands high enough. She attempted arching her back to throw her opponent off, but the woman simply settled farther back on her chest until Dantlinger collapsed back to the ground.

Black spots swam in her vision, but through the impending blackout and her rising panic, Dantlinger remembered a move her sensei had performed to free himself from a similar hold. She only hoped her legs were strong enough.

With the last of her energy, Dantlinger curled her abdomen as she brought her right leg up and around the woman's head. At its apogee, she brought it back down, her calf smacking into her opponent's face and driving her down onto her back. With the woman's center of gravity upset, Dantlinger was able to shove the constricting leg off her throat and suck in a life-giving breath of air.

The woman kept rolling with the move, throwing off Dantlinger's leg and kicking back into a reverse somersault, ending up on her hands and feet in a crouch. Her eyes darted to something on the ground beside her, and her hand shot out to grab her dagger. She stood up while Dantlinger knelt on the ground, still gasping for breath.

"That was cute, but now I'm gonna slash your throat. I wonder how your last kiss will taste, ranger girl."

She walked over behind Dantlinger and grabbed her by the hair, pulling her head back as she bent over, the knife coming down at her throat—

As Dantlinger came up, however, her hands were fisted around the SIG-Sauer pistol she'd drawn from her pocket. Jamming it into her attacker's stomach, she pulled the trigger twice.

The woman convulsed as the .40-caliber bullets tore through her intestines and kidneys. They continued their tumbling flight, shattering her lower vertebrae before punching two large holes out her back. She froze where she was, the knife dropping from her limp hand as she clutched her bloody torso. Her mouth opened and closed, but no words came out as she collapsed to the ground.

Massaging her aching throat, Dantlinger climbed to her feet, the smoking pistol still in her hand. She looked at the huddled, silent woman. "Guess that finally shut you the fuck up. If you're lucky, we might be back before you bleed out. If not, enjoy the last several hours of your agonizing life."

Retrieving her submachine gun, she walked back over and removed the radio from the injured woman's belt. Just then the pickup exploded in a fireball, sending the chassis into the air, the destroyed remains of the vehicle landing on the cab, crushing it. The detonation knocked Dantlinger backward, and she shielded her eyes from the conflagration.

Flipping channels on the radio, she tried to raise Cooper as she looked around once more before heading deeper into the forest to the south.

16

Bolan found himself pinned down in the pickup truck bed as bullets punched neat holes in the fender near his head. Although the decoy flare had allowed him to get out of the passenger compartment, he had almost immediately come under fire from both sides of the truck.

He rolled to the passenger side just as the sniper rifle's report boomed again in the distance and another round tore through the truck's driver side. The flames from the engine were also spreading backward, and soon would engulf the cargo bed or reach the gas tank. Neither one made for a case to stay put.

Sticking his subgun up over the side, Bolan cranked off several 3-round bursts on the right of the pickup. The firing intensified from that side, but had strangely stopped from the left. Bolan wasn't about to complain, however. Swapping magazines, he sprayed the forest on his right with two more bursts, then heaved himself over the right fender of the pickup, falling to the soft ground below.

The sniper rifle boomed again, and the passenger door spun off its remaining hinge and clattered to the ground. Bolan scooted underneath, hoping he could pick off at least one of the shooters before the sniper got lucky by firing through the truck again.

He scanned the forest, looking for any movement. Come on, where are you? He thought. The bullets didn't hit the truck from above, so they were still on the ground, but where?

He caught a flash of fire from the tree line about twenty yards behind the truck. It was followed by another burst of fire from another vector on the right side of the pickup. The right rear tire, miraculously undamaged so far, burst with a pop and hiss of escaping air.

Extending the stock of the HK gun, Bolan propped himself up on his elbows, his head scraping the gas tank, and aimed down the barrel at the tree the rearmost gunner was hiding behind. Through his night-vision goggles, he could see the barrel of the weapon the man was holding. Bolan steadied his breathing and concentrated on his target. But for some reason, the gunner wasn't taking another shot, instead choosing to stay under cover.

There was a whoosh from behind him as something pressurized in the engine burst with a spray of fluid. The flames dimmed for a moment, then flared up with renewed intensity. Bolan felt his feet and legs growing hotter each second. He could not wait any longer. Shutting everything else out, he narrowed his world to the dot inside the circle at the end of the gun, placing it squarely on the part of the enemy's weapon that he could see.

Amid the chaos going on all around him, Bolan inhaled through his nose, let the air escape through his mouth, then, when his body was at its most relaxed, he squeezed the trigger.

The 3-shot burst leaped from the barrel, impacting the weapon and the tree trunk in a spray of splinters. The submachine gun spun away as the gunman shouted in surprise and pain.

Bolan immediately turned his weapon toward the gunner on the right and emptied the magazine into the forest while crawling toward the back of the pickup. Once out from underneath, he scrambled to his feet and sprinted to the nearest trees on the right. A spray of bullets kicked up dirt around his feet as he dived for the cover of a trio of trees. No sooner had he hit the ground than the pickup truck exploded behind him. Bolan looked back to see the upside-down frame and chassis crash back to the ground, spraying pieces of metal and flames everywhere.

Once in the tree line, Bolan peeked out at the gunman's position behind him, then dashed to a tree about four yards away. No gunfire followed him this time, making Bolan wonder if the man had gotten hit by shrapnel or if he was just reloading. He removed the empty magazine from his own weapon and found another—his last one—in his coat pocket. Shoving it into the receiver, he pulled back the cocking lever and scanned the forest for targets.

His radio squawked. "Cooper? Cooper, you there?"

Crouching, Bolan grabbed it and turned the volume down. "Sarah, where are you?"

"Three o'clock from the pickup. I took one out. How about you?"

"There're still two running around, plus the sniper, so be careful. One was at nine, one at six, but he might only have a pistol now, I'm not sure."

"What's the plan?"

Aware that every word they were saying might be overheard. Bolan spoke fast. "Sweep south, and let's see if we can catch the rear gunner between us. If not, we'll meet in the middle."

"Roger."

Instead of heading south, however, Bolan remained where he was in the cluster of trees and brush, watching for movement from the north.

A HALF MILE TO THE NORTH, Chi had been having a grand time. The truck was a blazing pyre, but it looked like the two occupants had escaped, amazingly enough. He activated his headset mike.

"Chi to Lambda, over."

"This is Lambda," came the whispered reply. "Do you have line of sight on either of them?"

Chi ranged his scope over the forest surrounding the burning wreck. "No LOS on either target at this time, over. Can you give me a bearing?"

"I think so. Hang on a second." Novikov had made sure that every member of the strike force had learned extensive orienteering and fire control to serve as forward observers for their sniper. Hopefully Lambda and Chi could make it pay off in the next few minutes by splattering their target all over the forest.

"Okay. I'm in the pines two degrees west of your position. Do you see my infrared light?" A moment later, Chi saw a bright flash blink twice, then stop.

"Roger that, have confirmed your position."

"Roger that. Fire four degrees over and six hundred yards out, continuing in five-yard increments, over."

Chi had already replaced his half-full magazine with a full one. "Roger, commencing fire." He sighted in on his first aim point, breathed out and squeezed the trigger, riding the recoil and settling the big gun down to take his next shot.

FOLLOWING COOPER'S instructions, Dantlinger had headed south about fifty yards, then turned right and began creeping over until the still-burning hulk of the pickup was on her right side. She turned ninety degrees again and began picking her way through the forest, scanning for the southernmost gunman.

About ten yards into her search, she heard a rustle in the brush to her right. She turned that way, snugging the HK into her shoulder as she aimed toward the noise.

Too late, she sensed something large above and to her left. Dantlinger started to turn back in time to see a dark form leaping at her out of the trees—and then he was on her, knocking the subgun from her hands as he bowled her to the ground.

The park ranger rolled with the blow and came up on her feet, fingers scrabbling for her pistol. But the man was running away from her, heading straight for the dropped HK. He dived for it as Dantlinger snap-fired three shots at him, then took off into the trees as he turned on the ground and began peppering the woods near her with bullets.

Dantlinger bobbed and weaved, trying to put as many trees between her and the shooter as possible. The cracks and whines of bullets impacting tree trunks and branches sounded deafening in her ears, but she kept running, expecting to feel the punch of a bullet hitting her at any second.

After another thirty seconds, she took cover behind a huge ponderosa pine and grabbed her radio with a shaking hand. "Cooper? Cooper, come in—"

The thunder of the sniper rifle shattered the stillness around her, and Dantlinger crouched, wondering where those bullets were headed.

BOLAN WAS JUST ABOUT to leave his hiding place when the sniper let loose again. He heard the bullet drill into a nearby tree about ten yards ahead and to his right. As he hunkered down and watched, the sniper adjusted his aim and fired again, this bullet plowing through a tree parallel to Bolan's cover.

They're trying to flush me out, he thought. Slinging his weapon, Bolan began crawling west on his hands and knees, deeper into the forest. The booms of the sniper rifle echoed all around him, but none of the bullets came close. When he was twenty yards away from his hole, Bolan

ound a large tree and slowly stood up as his radio clicked
gain. "Cooper, Cooper, come in."

He clicked the radio once, then said, "Maintain radio
ilence—I'll come to you."

Examining the radio, he soon found its GPS tracking
rogram, which included locating the other radios in a
wo-mile radius. Reviewing the positions of the nearby
adios, he quickly memorized the sniper's position, and
narked where he thought the two remaining gunners were
n the ground. That left the last one as Dantlinger—he
oped.

Grabbing his subgun with both hands, Bolan ran west
or a bit, then cut south toward the farthest signal. When
e was within a hundred yards, he clicked the send button.
"Sarah, I'm approaching you from the north."

"We'll see if you really are. Keep coming, and I'll let
ou know one way or the other."

Shoulders hunched, Bolan kept going south as the sniper
ontinued firing in the distance. He'd gone about fifty
ards when he heard the click of a pistol safety.

"Hold it," a familiar voice said.

"Sarah, it's me, Cooper."

"Let that weapon fall and remove that mask so I can be
ure."

Bolan released the handle of the HK and let it dangle by
ts strap as he took off the night-vision goggles. The night
ir felt good on his sweaty skin. "Satisfied?"

"Yeah." Dantlinger stepped from the brush where she'd
een hiding. "We'd better go retrieve my radio. I left it
ifty yards that way."

"Clever, but if you figured out the GPS positioning, no
loubt our buddies will too." They started walking through
he brush. "What happened to your machine gun?"

"That fuckin' gunner in the south got the drop on me—
iterally, he came at me out of a damn tree. He knocked it

out of my hands and went for it instead of trying to clobbe
me. I tried to tag him with my pistol, but missed and bea
feet when the bullets started flying."

"Good thing you did, too. How many magazines do yo
have?"

"Just what's in the pipe—six rounds. What about you?"

"This is the last magazine. Everything else went up with
the Chevy. You got anything else on you?"

"Just a couple of flares and a bottle of water. Great
We're screwed."

"No, we've just got to get these two off our backs, and
I think I know how. Are there any cave systems around
here?"

"Yeah, there're several small ones in the hills to the
north, why?"

"If this works, we can lure our two chasers into a trap
Come on."

ALTERNATING JOGGING and walking, Bolan and Dantlinger
covered a mile and a half in about twenty minutes, leaving
a fairly obvious trail. Every so often, Bolan took a reading of where their pursuers were. "Yeah, they're about 250
yards back, following right behind us like dogs on a scent."

"Why don't we return the favor and try to ambush
them?"

"Because we don't have the ammo for a prolonged firefight, and although we're both pretty good shots, if we
didn't take them down immediately, we could find ourselves in a lot of trouble."

"The cave you're looking for should be up ahead. Back
in the day, rogue prospectors often sank test shafts around
here. They dot the mountains here and there."

They pushed through another copse of firs and came
into a small clearing that ended in a steeply slanting rock

face to the north. A dark hole, mostly overgrown with tall grass, gaped in the side of the rock.

"Let's take a quick look inside."

Every sense alert, Bolan led Dantlinger into the mine, ducking to avoid hitting his head on the thick wooden crossbeams. He made a conscious effort to slow his panting, aware of the detriment his injuries and the exertion were having on him at this altitude.

The normally pitch-black interior was lit by the eerie, lambent-green of his night-vision goggles. The mine headed straight back for ten yards, then forked off into two passageways. Bolan headed down each one for a few steps, then turned back. "Each of these looks fairly good. Give me your radio."

Dantlinger handed it over, and Bolan placed it a few yards down the leftmost passageway. As he came back, he suddenly felt a bit woozy and stopped to lean against the rough rock wall.

"Matt, hold up. Are you feeling all right?"

Bolan took stock of himself, checking his bandages for seepage or any other injures he might have missed. "I think so, but I just felt light-headed for a moment. Why?"

"I don't feel good—sort of logy, like my mind's getting fuzzy. I think we might be in a methane pocket."

Bolan knew a little about the naturally occurring, colorless, odorless gas, mainly how explosive it was in high concentrations. Although he couldn't smell anything, he was also becoming aware of the effect Dantlinger had mentioned. "We should get out, right?"

"Absolutely."

They retreated back up to the mine entrance. "Are you sure the radio is going to lure them in?" she asked.

Bolan's answering grin was wolfish. "I think we've got enough time to make them believe we went inside."

Trotting back to the nearest patch of dirt, he stirred

some up with his borrowed dagger, then poured out enough water from his canteen to create a puddle of mud. He took off his hiking boots and coated their soles in it. "Do the same with yours."

Once Dantlinger had covered her boot soles, they both walked in bare feet to where they had entered the clearing. Putting their boots on again, they made muddy prints on the rock leading into the cave, then, when they reached where Dantlinger had first sensed the gas, they took their boots off and trotted back out in bare feet.

The park ranger grimaced. "Damn, that's cold."

"Try hiking a couple miles in bare feet—*that's* cold." Bolan led her to a thick clump of brush and concealed them both behind it before putting their boots back on. "Shh—they should be here any second now."

His warning was very accurate. About a minute later, the lead EarthStrike ecoterrorist appeared at the edge of the clearing, scanning all around with his night-vision goggles. Bolan's shoulders hunched as the man's gaze passed over where they were hiding, but their cover was good, since he didn't spot them.

He spotted the tracks, however, and followed them to the mouth of the mine. Scanning around one more time, the man signaled to someone Bolan couldn't see and was joined moments later by the second attacker, each one carrying compact HK MP-5 A-3 submachine guns and holstered pistols. Bolan's hands ached to get a hold of any of those weapons. He considered Dantlinger's suggestion— trying to ambush them with the rounds they had left—but dismissed the idea. If they failed, then Dantlinger and he would be dead in short order. Getting to the bomb was still the primary mission. Getting these guys off their backs almost as important, but still secondary.

The men spoke briefly, then the lead scout headed into the mine, followed a few paces back by his backup.

Bolan gave them a twenty-second head start, then nudged Dantlinger. "Give me one of your flares."

She handed one over, and Bolan crept to the mouth of the mine. He crept about five yards in, then struck the flare against its igniter, turning his face away to avoid being blinded by the sudden glare.

The flare sparked immediately, its red-white flame lighting the narrow tunnel. Bolan heard voices from deeper inside, but he didn't wait for them to come back and investigate. Cocking his arm, he hurled the lit flare as far inside as he could, then turned to run back for the entrance, mouth open and hands covering his ears.

Almost instantly there was an even brighter flash from deep within the tunnel, followed a second later by a skull-cracking explosion that picked Bolan up and hurled him out of the mine. He tucked and rolled, aware of the blast of heat and huge tongue of red-gold flame erupting from the entrance all around him. Covering his face, Bolan kept rolling, making sure any lingering flames on him were put out. As he extinguished himself, he became aware of a larger rumbling and felt a pair of hands pulling him away.

"Come on! Come on!" Dantlinger shouted. Bolan got to his feet and staggered away as the rumbling grew even louder. Looking back, he saw his improvised trap had been a little too successful.

The mine entrance had collapsed from the explosion, sending a plume of dirt and dust high into the air. The opening to the tunnel had become a jumbled pile of stones and boulders, burying the two ecoterrorists under several tons of dirt and rock. Bolan looked at the destruction. "Well, that's one way to take care of them. Damn shame about the weapons, though."

Dusting himself off, he eyed the rock face of the bluff. "Let's go. We've got a sniper to find."

17

"It's smaller than I thought it would be."

Novikov and his five remaining men stood at the edge of Mary Lake. Surrounded by rock bluffs, calling the small body of water a lake was more of an act of charity than anything else, Novikov mused. Still, the surveys Beta had conducted had told him that this was the best place to set off the warhead, so this was where it would be placed and detonated.

He turned to the rest of his men. "Our mission is almost complete."

"Have we received word from the others yet?" Tau asked.

Novikov shook his head. They had heard many gunshots as they were making their final approach to the lake, along with a fairly large explosion, but since then the forest behind them had been eerily quiet. "I hope they have been successful, but we cannot wait for confirmation of their mission. However…"

He turned and scanned the slope of the bluff overlooking the lake. "Delta, Upsilon, take the second long rifle and head back about a half mile to the top of that bluff and make sure no one's coming to surprise us. The rest of you begin assembling the boats."

The other three began taking off long, flat pieces of polypropylene and placing them on the ground. Flipping up the sides, they then attached hard plastic seats. Soon a fourteen-foot boat was sitting on the ground. The folding boats were lightweight, portable and incredibly sturdy—the perfect vehicles for carrying the team and the warhead out to the middle of the lake.

Novikov walked to a storage compartment on the six-wheeled transport. Opening it, he removed a small backpack and went back to the warhead on the second trailer. Holding a penlight in his teeth, he unzipped the backpack and removed a small, self-contained, waterproof electric timer. Opening the hull of the warhead, he began the delicate task of wiring in the timer to the arming and detonation mechanism of the weapon. He followed every memorized step carefully, his steady hands making the connections and carefully testing the power source.

All I need is just a few more minutes, he thought. *And then no one can stop us.*

DANTLINGER CREPT FORWARD, each of her steps on the carpet of pine needles sounding like thunder in her ears. Her pistol was heavy in her hand, her index finger trembling only slightly as she crept forward. She tried to remember her martial-arts training, which had taught her to keep her breathing steady and to place her feet with deliberation, but at the moment all she knew was that her throat was sore, her nerves were on edge, and somewhere up ahead of her was the sniper they'd been stalking for the better part of ten minutes.

After the mine collapse, they'd climbed the rock bluff and headed east, following the lone GPS signal they were still picking up in the immediate area. When they were a quarter-mile away, Bolan had stopped and hunkered down. After gulping more water, he outlined the plan.

"Okay, if this signal is correct, the sniper's about five hundred yards ahead. We should split up and come at him from two different directions, giving one of us a better chance of actually taking him by surprise. I'll circle to the north and come in from behind, you continue on this route and try to take him from here. Now listen. If you get a shot on him, you take it, don't wait and definitely don't try to take him alive."

Although she had thought there was a better chance of one of them getting killed, she had nodded. "Don't worry about that. What if one of us gets killed before we get up on him?"

"He should be armed with only the pistol and the rifle. If he takes out one of us and the survivor doesn't believe they can eliminate him, they should try to keep moving and eliminate the rest of the group if possible. Any questions?"

At the time, she'd shaken her head, and they had split up. However, being alone in the forest, with only the gibbous moon overhead for company, she thought this was an even dumber idea. Part of her wanted to contact her partner and abort the whole thing, but he'd told her to keep strict radio silence once they were apart. Swallowing around the softball-sized lump in her throat, the ranger kept moving forward.

A particularly large thicket of trees blocked her vision, and Dantlinger carefully got on her hands and knees to crawl underneath it, figuring it would provide cover as well as let her see out. She wormed forward on her chest, staying as low to the ground as possible. She smelled the unmistakable scent of pine trees and the earth all around her. Wriggling past two trunks that had grown close together, she crawled underneath a fallen tree and peeked out under a low-hanging branch—

Holy shit—he's right in front of me! her mind screamed.

Dantlinger froze, not daring to even breathe. About eight feet ahead of her was a mound of cut tree branches, camouflaging a prone human form, with the long barrel of the sniper rifle poking out, aimed at the valley below. On the other end, a pair of combat boots lay on the ground, covered by another cut tree branch.

Dantlinger looked down at the pistol in her hand, which was flat against the ground. Slowly she lifted it, an inch at a time, until it was in front of her. Careful not to make a sound, she extended the SIG-Sauer until it was pointed straight at the figure ahead. Gritting her teeth, she lined up the sights on its middle mass and squeezed the trigger twice.

The pistol's reports thundered in the silence. One of the tree branches broke in two and fell over, and the form underneath seemed to deflate a bit. Keeping her pistol trained on the body, Sarah crawled out and moved to the figure. Tossing away branches, she revealed—

A backpack? She whirled—to stare into the barrel of a pistol aimed at her face. The man behind it was very tall and thin, his face painted in camouflage stripes of green, brown and black.

"Don't move."

Dantlinger obeyed, not even raising her hands.

"Drop the pistol."

The park ranger set her gun down, wondering anxiously where her partner was. She weighed the possibility of lunging at the man to get her hands on the pistol. As if reading her mind, he took a step backward. "Where's your partner?"

"Dead. He was hit on the way out of the truck, bled out somewhere in the woods down there."

"Then you are of no more use to me either." He tightened his grip on the pistol, aiming it at her head.

Dantlinger tensed for the bullet and closed her eyes, hoping it would kill her before she knew it.

A gunshot split the night, followed immediately by the sniper's pistol cracking, and something stinging her ear. Dantlinger cautiously opened her eyes to see the man standing there, a vacant look in his eyes, the smoking pistol in his hand pointed at the ground. He toppled forward, landing face-first next to her. She reached over and grabbed the pistol from his limp hand, then saw that the back of his head was a bloody ruin. Touching her fingers to her ear, they came back wet and black in the moonlight. *Jesus, he almost killed me,* she thought.

"Cooper? Cooper?" she whispered, grabbing her own pistol and holding one in each hand, aiming them both into the darkness. "Where the hell are you?"

She heard muffled footsteps and a moment later Bolan appeared out of the brush. "Sorry I cut that so close. I wanted to make sure I didn't hit you, which meant a head shot."

She shook her head, gulping down huge breaths. "No, that's all right." She showed him her hand. "He did almost blow my head off, and I almost fucking wet myself, but I'm still alive, and that's what matters."

Bolan was already moving, clearing the cut brush and revealing the long, wicked-looking sniper rifle. He quickly checked it over. "Any more bullets in his gear?"

Dantlinger pulled his pack apart looking. "One more full magazine." Finding a small first-aid kit, she made a quick bandage for her damaged earlobe. "Ow, that stings."

"Better than the alternative."

Despite the gallows humor, Dantlinger smiled back, just glad to be alive. "That's for damn sure."

"At least he didn't disable his weapon." Bolan ejected the magazine. "Six rounds left, sixteen total. That ought to be more than enough." Handing the HK subgun to

Dantlinger, he picked up the heavy weapon. "As I see it, there's at least five or six of them left. While I'd love to get on that high ridge up there, I bet that's where at least two of them have established an overlook to watch for us, and we can't waste the time finding them."

"So we go around?"

"Exactly. Hope you're in shape, 'cause we'll be moving as fast as we can."

"What if we come under fire on the way?"

"Take cover and return it if you can. Now let's move out."

"HELL OF A VIEW up here." Concealed behind a tree, Delta swept the forest below with his third generation night-vision binoculars. The only African American of the group, he had been a climate scientist who had gotten tired of banging the global warming drum and had joined Earth-Strike to make a statement that no one around the world could ignore. Despite never having seen a dead person until yesterday, he'd handled it very well, and after emptying his stomach, he was ready to complete the mission, no matter how many bodies they had to leave behind.

"Got that right. I'm surprised we can't see all the way back to the campsite from here." Lying on the ground, Upsilon, a lanky Southerner, and the next best sharpshooter after Chi, made one more adjustment to the scope on his own .50-caliber Bushmaster rifle. "Rough sighted in for four hundred yards. Really wish I could of taken a rangin' shot."

"Well, you just might get your chance. I've got movement in the trees at eight o'clock." Delta picked up his radio and turned it to the most recent channel on their assigned schedule. "Lambda, Zeta, Epsilon, Chi, come on. Lambda, Zeta, Epsilon, Chi—anyone out there?"

Delta and Upsilon exchanged glances.

"Not answering—they definitely ain't friendly," Upsilon said as he inserted a magazine and rammed the bolt forward to chamber a round. Delta adjusted his night vision binoculars to try and zero in on the pair running through the sparse woods several hundred yards below.

Upsilon adjusted for altitude and wind. "Ready when you are, Delta."

Through the binoculars, his spotter gave him coordinates for the first bullet placement—or thereabouts. "We'll have to adjust on the fly."

"What else is new?" Upsilon lined up the crosshairs, steadied himself, exhaled and squeezed the trigger.

FOUR-HUNDRED and fifty-eight yards away, Bolan and Dantlinger were darting from tree to tree when he stumbled, going to one knee. At that exact moment, the small tree a yard ahead cracked and burst apart. It was followed immediately by the rolling boom of a .50-caliber rifle.

"Sniper! Down!" Bolan continued his downward trajectory by the simple expedient of falling forward on his face. He quickly crawled onward until he was behind another tree. "Sarah, get to cover!"

"Believe me, I'm already there," she called out from behind another tree a few yards away. Another round smashed into the tree above Bolan's head, raining bark and branches down on him. Unslinging the rifle, the soldier rolled right and tried to sight in on where the sniper was firing from.

"I've got the coordinates, but I can't determine a good angle. The trees on the slope don't help either. There's only one thing to do."

"I'm listening!"

"I'm going to spray that bluff with several rounds. Hopefully keep their heads down. The moment I start firing, you take off and get around the bluff. I'll follow as soon as I can."

"I can't shoot back?"

"Your weapon doesn't have the range. You've got to get to the lake. Ready?"

"Ready!"

"On my mark!" Bolan waited for the next roar of the enemy sniper, then he rolled out six feet and rose to one knee. Aiming the heavy weapon at the bluff, he squeezed off a shot, worked the bolt and shot again. "Go, go, go!"

Dantlinger took off behind him, arms pumping and legs churning for all she was worth.

An answering shot kicked up dirt three feet from him, and Bolan adjusted his aim on the fly and shot twice more before getting to his feet and also running like a madman across the rock scree.

"WHOO-EE! THAT WAS a close one, wasn't it Delta?" Upsilon squinted through his scope as he tried to find either one of the targets. "Gimme a vector, and I'll nail that son of a bitch this time. Delta?"

He looked up to see no one standing above him. "Delta, you get tagged?" Looking behind him, he saw the spotter's motionless body sprawled on the ground, his chest a mass of blood and wood splinters. Upsilon looked at the tree Delta had been standing behind, which sported a fresh inch-wide hole through the trunk, with a fist-sized exit wound.

"Goddamn." Upsilon gently closed Delta's sightless eyes. "All right, ya sons a bitches, I'm a'comin' for ya." Shucking most of his gear, he took all the ammunition he could carry and loped off in the direction his targets had been running.

BOLAN AND DANTLINGER scrambled across the slope, trying to maintain their balance as best as they could on the uneven surface. The soldier led the way, aiming for a break in the hillside that would allow them to look down upon the lake.

"Hey, the sniper's on the move!" Dantlinger said behind him. "Look!"

Bolan checked the radio. Sure enough, one of the two signals from the top of the bluff was heading straight for them. "Well, that's unexpected."

"Is that all you have to say?"

"Nope. It sure isn't what I would have done in his place." Bolan levered another huge shell into the Bushmaster's barrel. "Go out twenty yards on my right flank and pace me. I'm going to take the high ground. When I see him, I'll engage to distract him. You close in on his flank and take him out if I haven't. Go!"

Dantlinger slid down the hillside a bit and took her position. Bolan watched the tiny blip on the radio approach, then started walking up the hill. "Okay, sniper, let's dance."

UPSILON DUG HIS HEELS into the loose scree and rocks as he came charging down the hillside, scanning back and forth for the bastard who had taken out Delta. He figured he was more than halfway to the last position of the shooter, and corrected to head a bit more northwesterly.

He was approaching a cluster of firs when a booming shot rang out, and a tree broke in two and fell to the ground in front of him. Upsilon kept moving, gathering speed and leaping over the fallen trunk. The moment he touched ground, he fell backward onto his butt so he was sitting and propped his elbows on his knees as he followed the trajectory of the bullet back along its path. He saw movement behind a tree trunk, aimed and fired, yanking back the bolt to chamber another round. Hoisting the rifle up to his shoulder again, he took a look at the blasted tree in his crosshairs.

"I got you now, you son of a—"

Fire burst behind his eyes, and everything went black for Upsilon.

TEN YARDS AWAY, Dantlinger knelt on the ground, still sighting along the HK MP-5's barrel. The 3-round burst had gone precisely where she'd aimed—the side of the target's head.

It had been surprisingly easy. The sniper had been so intent on his target that he hadn't even been checking his perimeter for other enemies. She rose to her feet as Bolan strode up the hill toward her.

"Now what? We keep going around?"

"Nope. Grab that other rifle. We're cutting across here and taking up a position above them. We'll have both the high ground and the weapons that will outmatch anything they can bring to bear against us. If I can shoot all of them from five hundred yards out, I'm sure as hell going to. Let's go."

18

The rifle shots echoed like thunder around the bowl of the lake. Except for the occasional glance up toward the bluff, the rest of his men continued working, much to Novikov's satisfaction.

With the timer securely in place, he supervised the launching, then the loading of the boats, carefully transferring the warhead from the trailer to the second fourteen-foot foldable boat, which accepted the weight, still floating with several inches of gunwale to spare.

The rifle spoke once more above them, followed by the brief chatter of a submachine gun before everything fell silent. "Upsilon and Delta must have succeeded in removing that thorn in our side," he said to chuckles from the other three men around him. "They should be reporting in any moment now. Let's finalize the preparations."

He turned back to the two boats, gazing on the package containing the deliverance of the planet. His men were clearing up debris and putting their equipment away—not that it would matter in the next several minutes. Novikov signaled to the others. "Everyone take your positions in the boats." He raised his radio to his lips. "Delta, Upsilon, report—"

He heard a strange thunk and turned to see Xi fall to the

ground, clutching the stump of what had been his leg at the thigh as he screamed in agony. The shot rolled around them again, and Novikov knew instinctively what had happened.

"The warhead! We must launch the warhead!" he said, running to the boat, which had been grounded on the rock shelf that protruded into the water. Another shot blurred by, and another man fell, his head partly removed from his shoulders. Novikov pushed at the bow with all of his might, the last man left falling in beside him to move the boat into deeper water.

"Get in, get in and get the motor running!" Novikov kept pushing as his man scrambled over the warhead casing to the back of the boat. He prepped the small 10-horsepower motor and had just pulled the cord when lead and thunder rained down on them again.

As the report seared Novikov's ears, he felt something spatter his face. He looked up to see his last man fall into the water, clutching at the gaping hole in his chest. He looked down to see himself covered in blood, skin and viscera.

The boat was floating free, and Novikov pushed it farther out into the water and climbed aboard, moving to the side of the warhead that faced the lake. He slid to the back of the vessel, only to find out that the bullet that had gone through his man had smashed into the engine as well, rendering it useless.

No matter! I will not be denied—not this close to completion! Novikov vowed. He unfastened the motor and dumped the useless weight overboard. Taking cover behind the warhead itself, he grabbed a paddle from the bottom of the boat and began stroking for the middle of the lake.

"WHAT'S THE MATTER? Take the shot!" Dantlinger said.

"Can't risk holing the boat. We have to go after him. Come on!"

Leaping to his feet, Bolan ran down the bluff slope and across the loose rock to the shelf where Alpha and his men had been setting up their payload of destruction. Another strange-looking boat was sitting in the water, and Bolan sprinted for it. "Come on!"

Grabbing some straps lying on the ground, Dantlinger threw them inside and climbed in. Bolan yanked on the starter cord, making the engine splutter to life, and he twisted the throttle, aiming straight for the other boat, which was approaching the middle of the tiny lake.

Novikov looked over his shoulder to see the man and woman who had dogged his steps all night racing toward him in the second boat. Yanking his HK P-7 from its shoulder holster, he crouched behind the warhead and emptied the magazine at them. He knew they wouldn't dare shoot back and risk hitting the warhead.

Looking around, he saw he was close enough to the middle. He stood, opened the casing and activated the timer, starting the five-minute countdown.

Now all I have to do is sink this in the lake and my victory will be complete, he thought. The Russian stared at the pistol in his hand, and a wicked smile appeared on his face.

"He's doing something with the warhead!" Dantlinger called from where she had ducked low in the bow to avoid the bullets being shot at them.

"I see it! Come back and take the rudder!" Bolan crouched in the stern until the park ranger reached him, then he gave her the handle. "Head straight for him!"

"What? You mean ram him?"

"Exactly!"

"That's insane! If the warhead goes to the bottom, we're fucked!"

"Just keep going straight at him!" Bolan had the HK

MP-5 tight to his shoulder and tried to draw a bead on the last EarthStrike member. The motion of the boat made it hard to aim, and eventually he gave up, just as he noticed that they were going to cross in front of the other boat and its cargo.

"Closer! Get me closer!" Slinging his HK, Bolan stepped up into the prow as Dantlinger adjusted her course. They were about to pass within a few feet of the other boat's front. Bolan tensed, and then, when they were next to each other, he leaped onto the boat with the warhead just as several pistol shots went off.

NOVIKOV HAD JUST PUT several holes into the bottom of his boat when the entire craft rocked as if something had slammed into it just as the slide of his gun locked back. He ejected the magazine and had just grabbed a full one when the boat, already settling lower in the water, rocked dangerously. The Russian looked up to see a man in camouflage climbing over the top of the warhead. Inserting the magazine into the butt, he cycled the action and brought the gun up as the man brought a submachine gun around and aimed it at him.

Ducking underneath the curved body of the warhead, the ex-Spetsnaz commando stuck his pistol back up and fired several rounds at where his assailant had been. His shots were answered by a couple of 3-round bursts, but Novikov was already moving by then, ducking underneath the nose cone of the warhead to come up on the other side, leading with his pistol to take out his opponent.

But the man wasn't there. The hum of an approaching motor alerted him that the other intruder was coming back on his side. Novikov aimed his pistol at the approaching sound, waiting for the boat to come into view. A moment later, it did, and he heard the person at the tiller shout and point something at him as he unloaded his magazine at his enemy. The target slumped over and the boat turned away.

Sensing motion on the other side of the settling boat, the Russian slipped over the side into the water. Taking a deep breath and gripping his pistol in his mouth, he submerged and began pulling himself under the hull.

"SARAH! ARE YOU ALL RIGHT?" Bolan had heard her shout of "He's over here!" followed by several pistol shots, and then the sound of the engine on the other boat growing fainter.

The water was rising in the bottom of the boat, covering the toes of his combat boots, and Bolan knew he was running out of time. But the last man was still around, and he didn't dare turn his attention to the bomb while his enemy was lurking somewhere.

But where? Bolan tried to shut out the noise of the other engine, the steady bubble of water coming in at his feet, and the knowledge that he had less than four minutes to kill the last EarthStrike member and disarm the bomb. But first he had to figure out where he would likely be coming from.

The bubbling noise stopped for a moment, and Bolan's eyes widened as he realized where the man was—under the boat. Putting his back to the warhead, the soldier scanned the black, still lake, aiming with his HK and looking for the smallest disturbance on the water.

CAREFULLY, NOVIKOV pulled himself up onto the stern of the sinking boat. The big American was off on the far side of his vessel. He set his pistol down, knowing he'd never reload it in time to shoot the man. Instead he drew his Ostblock ballistic dagger and pulled the firing pin. Easing around the rear of the warhead, he edged farther out until he could see part of the head of his opponent. Novikov made sure of his footing, then leaned out even farther, aiming the knife at his target's chest and depressing the firing stud.

SENSING MOVEMENT on his right, Bolan brought the MP-5 around in time to see the last man aiming a double-edged dagger at him. With a shock of recognition, he squeezed the trigger even as the man launched the spring-loaded blade at him. Bolan tried to twist out of the way, but the blade still stabbed him in the bicep, plunging in to its metal hilt. The other unfortunate consequence of his move was that his bullets went wide of their mark, and then the HK clicked on an empty chamber.

The terrorist was already coming at him, another dagger in his hand. Bolan threw the empty gun at him, which the ecoterrorist dodged, then pulled the dagger blade out of his arm and hurled it back at his opponent, nailing him in the shoulder.

"Now we're even," Bolan snarled. The man didn't stop, but simply tossed his blade from his right hand to his left and charged forward. The Executioner tried to smash his opponent's face with his uninjured arm, but the guy simply took it on his forehead and slammed into Bolan, sending them both over the side of the boat into the icy lake water.

IN THE SECOND BOAT, Dantlinger groggily stirred in the bottom and tried to sit up. Her left arm hurt like hell when she moved it, and glancing down, she saw it was bleeding heavily.

"Shit, he got me!" She fumbled for the sniper's first-aid kit and tore it open, searching for a bandage and adhesive tape. Glancing up as she grabbed it, she saw that the boat was headed straight for the opposite shore.

Dammit, I'm gonna run aground! she thought. Grabbing the tiller, she pushed it hard right, sending the boat heeling over in a wide turn, narrowly missing the shore. She powered down and took a minute to wrap her bloody flesh wound. Although it hurt to move, she didn't think she'd broken any bones.

Once she was done, Dantlinger glanced at the warhead boat just in time to see Bolan fall into the water, with the last EarthStrike member on top of him. They thrashed about for a few seconds, then sank below the surface of the lake. Dantlinger's immediate attention, however, was caught by the other boat, which was definitely settling in the water, and taking the white cone with it.

Gunning the engine, the park ranger sent her vessel speeding back toward the sinking boat. When she got close, she pulled alongside and tried to figure out what to do—despite not knowing the first thing about warheads.

Shifting her feet in her boat, Dantlinger kicked the straps she had grabbed earlier back on the shore. Keeping hope that they were long enough, she grabbed the ends of the two straps and got to work.

BESIDES DROWNING, the immediate threat was the other man's dagger. Bolan had made sure to block the downward stab his adversary had tried to complete while tackling him, and now had the man's knife hand in a vise-like grip. That didn't limit his offensive capabilities, however, as he brought up his legs and tried to wrap them around his opponent's head. The other man snaked his injured arm in between them before Bolan could complete his scissor lock, and levered his legs apart before aiming an elbow at Bolan's groin. Twisting his waist, the soldier blocked the attack, all the while grinding on the man's wrist bones to make him drop the knife.

His lungs starting to burn, Bolan twisted the knife arm until the dagger popped free and fell into the dark water. Letting go of the man's hand, he grabbed at his throat while wrapping his legs around the man's waist, this time getting the lock in place at his ankles and tightening his thighs to expel any remaining oxygen from his opponent's lungs.

The man tried for an eye gouge, but all he did was dislodge Bolan's night vision goggles, which also fell into the lake. He clawed at the soldier's face again, but Bolan trapped his good hand and held him. The man's struggles grew more frantic as his air lessened, then, with a final, convulsive shudder, his mouth opened, and he spasmed as water flooded his lungs.

Although his own lungs were burning for air, Bolan held his leg lock on his adversary for another thirty seconds, until he was sure the man was dead. Only then did he release him and swim for the surface, blowing what little air remained in his lungs out until red-and-black spots danced in his vision, and he was on the verge of passing out. Heedless of the agony in his arm, Bolan kicked and clawed up one last time.

With a large splash, his head and shoulders broke the surface of the water, and he sucked in a huge gulp of clean, fresh mountain air. He leaned backward, keeping his head above water as he filled his lungs again.

"Cooper, help me!" The cry made him turn his head to see Dantlinger in the second boat about ten yards away. The warhead dangled half-in, half-out of the water, precariously strapped to her boat by a knotted series of tie-downs. "It's secure for now, but if it's gonna detonate by a timer, there's maybe a minute left!"

Bolan swam over to her and the warhead, searching for the access panel. He found it exactly where he didn't want to see it. "It's underneath—hold on." Sucking in a large gulp of air, he submerged, pushing himself into the black water. Feeling by touch alone, he located the panel, which was bisected by one of the straps holding it in place.

Bolan shoved the strap over, and opened the panel. Blinking red lights flashed in the darkness, the timer reading *21...20...19...18...*

Bolan tried to see if there was any kind of fail-safe, but he heard a slithering, and one side of the warhead starting sinking deeper into the lake. The strap was coming loose. He grabbed the edge of the cowling as the warhead slipped free of the remaining strap and began sinking to the bottom, taking Bolan with it.

Pressure began building in his ears as the soldier traced the wires connecting the timer to the detonation mechanism. *I hope this works,* he thought, as he grabbed them and pulled them free. The timer kept counting down—*7...6...5...4...*

Bolan grabbed every wire attached to the timer he could find and pulled them free, watching the final seconds tick away—*3...2...1...0.*

The timer flashed zero...and nothing happened. The bomb had been disarmed.

Bolan released the housing of the warhead and let it sink into the depths as he pushed for the surface again. He was moving more slowly this time, and wasn't sure he was going to reach it. His lungs strained for air, and he was just about to open his mouth when he felt a strong hands go under his shoulders and pull him up to the surface.

Bolan floated there, turning his head to see Dantlinger's dripping face smiling back at him. "Holy shit, you're alive!"

"Hey, so are you!" Bolan was about to say something else, but his words were cut off as Dantlinger pulled him close and kissed him hard. Surprised, all he could do was respond the best way he knew how—by kissing her back.

They pulled apart after a few seconds, a blush spreading over the park ranger's features. "Sorry about that. I'm just thrilled to be alive."

"You and me both, Ranger Dantlinger." Bolan hauled her close and kissed her again. "Now let's get the hell out of this freezing lake and in front of a roaring fire."

*****

TAKE 'EM FREE
2 action-packed novels plus a mystery bonus

NO RISK
NO OBLIGATION TO BUY

James Axler
Outlanders®

DRAGON CITY

**A vengeful enemy plots
a horrifying new assault on humanity.**

A cruel alien race, the Annunaki, has been reborn in a new and
more horrifying form. Enlil, cruelest of them all, is set to revive the
sadistic pantheon that will rule the Earth. Based in his Dragon City,
Enlil plans to create infinite gods—at the cost of humankind. With
the Cerberus team at its lowest ebb, can they possibly stop his
twisted plan?

Available May wherever books are sold.

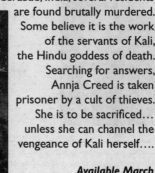